JOINING CHARLES

and other stories

'BETTER DRINK THIS,' SAID AGATHA

ELIZABETH BOWEN

JOINING CHARLES

and other stories

JONATHAN CAPE
THIRTY BEDFORD SQUARE
LONDON

FIRST PUBLISHED 1929
FIRST PUBLISHED IN THE COLLECTED EDITION 1952

ISBN   0224 600621

PRINTED IN GREAT BRITAIN IN THE CITY OF OXFORD
AT THE ALDEN PRESS
BOUND BY A. W. BAIN & CO. LTD., LONDON

CONTENTS

JOINING CHARLES

and other stories

JOINING CHARLES

EVERYBODY in the White House was awake early that morning, even the cat. At an unprecedented hour in the thick grey dusk Polyphemus slipped upstairs and began to yowl at young Mrs. Charles's door, under which came out a pale yellow line of candle-light. On an ordinary morning he could not have escaped from the kitchen so easily, but last night the basement door had been left unbolted; all the doors were open downstairs, for the household had gone to bed at a crisis of preparation for the morrow. Sleep was to be no more than an interim, and came to most of them thinly and interruptedly. The rooms were littered with objects that had an air of having been put down momentarily, corded boxes were stacked up in the hall, and a spectral breakfast-table waiting all night in the parlour reappeared slowly as dawn came in through the curtains.

Young Mrs. Charles came across to the door on her bare feet, and, shivering, let in Polyphemus. She was still in pyjamas, but her two suitcases were packed to the brim, with tissue paper smoothed on the tops of them: she must have been moving about for hours. She was always, superstitiously, a little afraid of Polyphemus and made efforts to propitiate him on all occasions; his expression of omniscience had imposed upon her thoroughly. His coming in now made her a little conscious; she stood still, one hand on the knob of the dressing-table drawer, and put the other hand to her forehead – what must she do? Between the curtains, drawn a little apart, light kept coming in slowly, solidifying the objects round her, which till now had been uncertain, wavering silhouettes in candle-light. So night fears gave place to the realities of daytime.

Polyphemus continued to melt round the room, staring malignly at nothing. Presently Agatha tapped and came in in her dressing-gown; her plaits hung down each side of her long, kind face, and she carried a cup of tea.

'Better drink this,' said Agatha. 'What can I do?' She drew back the curtains a little more in her comfortable, common-sense way to encourage the daylight. Leaning for a moment out of the window she breathed in critically the morning air; the bare upland country was sheathed but not hidden by mist. 'You're going to have a beautiful day,' said Agatha.

Mrs. Charles shivered, then began tugging a comb through her short hair. She had been awake a long time and felt differently from Agatha about the day; she looked at her sister-in-law haggardly. 'I dreamed and dreamed,' said Mrs. Charles. 'I kept missing my boat, saw it sliding away from the quay; and when I turned to come back to you all England was sliding away too, in the other direction, and I don't know where I was left – and I dreamed, too, of course, about losing my passport.'

'One would think you had never travelled before,' said Agatha tranquilly. She sat down on the end of the narrow bed where Mrs. Charles had slept for the last time, and shaking out Mrs. Charles's garments, passed them to her one by one, watching her dress as though she had been a child. Mrs. Charles felt herself being marvelled at; her own smallness and youth had become objective to her at the White House; a thing, all she had, to offer them over again every day to be softened and pleased by.

As she pulled on the clothes she was to wear for so long she began to feel formal and wary, the wife of a competent banker going to join him at Lyons. The expression of her feet in those new brogues was quite unfamiliar: the feet of a 'nice little woman'. Her hair, infected by this feeling of strangeness that flowed to her very extremities, lay in a different line against her head. For a moment the face of a ghost from the future stared at her out of the looking-glass. She turned quickly to Agatha, but her sister-in-law had left her while she was buttoning her jumper at the neck and had gone downstairs to print some more labels. It had occurred to Agatha that there would be less chance of losing the luggage (a contingency by which this untravelled family seemed to be haunted) if Louise were to tie on new labels, with more explicit directions, at Paris, where she would have to re-register. Agatha was gone, and the cup of tea, untasted, grew cold on the dressing-table.

The room looked bare without her possessions and withdrawn, as though it had already forgotten her. At this naked hour of parting she had forgotten it also; she supposed it would come back in retrospect so distinctly as to be a kind of torment. It was a smallish room with sloping ceilings, and a faded paper rambled over by roses. It had white curtains and was never entirely dark; it had so palpably a life of its own that she had been able to love it with intimacy and a sense of return, as one could never have loved an inanimate thing. Lying in bed one could see from the one window nothing but sky or sometimes a veil of rain; when one got up and looked out there were fields, wild and bare, and an unbroken skyline to emphasize the security of the house.

The room was up on the top floor, in one of the gables; a big household cannot afford a spare bedroom of any pretensions. To go downstairs one had to unlatch the nursery gate at the head of the top flight. Last time Charles was home it had been very unfortunate; he had barked his shins on the gate and shouted angrily to his mother to know what the thing was *still* there for. Louise fully realized that it was being kept for Charles's children.

During that first visit with Charles she had hardly been up to the second floor, where the younger girls slept in the old nursery. There had been no confidences; she and Charles occupied very connubially a room Mrs. Ray gave up to them that had been hers since her marriage. It was not till Louise came back here alone that the White House opened its arms to her and she began to be carried away by this fullness, this intimacy and queer seclusion of family life. She and the girls were in and out of each other's rooms; Doris told sagas of high school, Maisie was always just on the verge of a love-affair, and large grave Agatha began to drop the formality with which she had greeted a married woman and sister-in-law. She thought Agatha would soon have forgotten she was anything but her own child if it had ever been possible for Agatha to forget Charles.

It would have been terrible if Louise had forgotten, as she so nearly had, to pack Charles's photograph. There it had stood these three months, propped up on the mantelpiece, a handsome convention in sepia, becomingly framed, from which the young wife, falling asleep or waking, had turned away her face instinctively.

She folded back a layer of tissue paper before shutting her suitcase and poked down a finger to feel the edge of the frame and reassure herself. There it was, lying face down, wrapped up in her dressing-gown, and she would have seen Charles before she looked again at his photograph. The son and brother dominating the White House would be waiting on Lyons platform to enfold her materially.

Mrs. Charles glanced round the room once more, then went downstairs slowly. Through the house she could hear doors opening and shutting and people running about because of her. She felt ashamed that her packing was finished and there was nothing for her to do. Whenever she had pictured herself leaving the White House it had been in the evening, with curtains drawn, and they had all just come out to the door for a minute to say goodbye to her, then gone back to the fire. It had been more painful but somehow easier. Now she felt lonely; they had all gone away from her, there was nobody there.

She went shyly into the morning-room as though for the first time and knelt down on the rug in front of a young fire. There was a sharp smell of wood-smoke; thin little flames twisted and spat through the kindling. A big looking-glass, down to the ground, reflected her kneeling there; small and childish among the solemn mahogany furniture; more like somebody sent back to school than someone rejoining a virile and generous husband who loved her. Her cropped fair hair turned under against her cheek and was cut in a straight line over the eyebrows. She had never had a home before, and had been able to boast till quite lately that she had never been homesick. After she married there had been houses in which she lived with Charles, but still she had not known what it meant to be homesick.

She hoped that, after all, nobody would come in for a moment or two; she had turned her head and was looking out at the lawn with its fringe of trees not yet free from the mist, and at the three blackbirds hopping about on it. The blackbirds made her know all at once what it meant to be going away; she felt as though someone had stabbed her a long time ago but she were only just feeling the knife. She could not take her eyes from the blackbirds, till one with a wild flutey note skimmed off into the trees and the other two followed it. Polyphemus had come in after her and was looking out at them, pressing himself against the window-pane.

'Polyphemus,' said Mrs. Charles in her oddly unchildish voice, 'have you any illusions?' Polyphemus lashed his tail.

By midday (when she would be nearly at Dover) the fire would be streaming up briskly, but by that time the sun would be pouring in at the windows and no one would need a fire at all. The mornings were not cold yet, the girls were active, and it was only because of her going away that the fire had been lighted. Perhaps Agatha, who never hurt anything's feelings, would come in and sit not too far away from it with her basket of mending, making believe to be glad of the heat. 'I don't suppose there'll be fires at Lyons,' thought Mrs. Charles. Somewhere, in some foreign room tomorrow evening when the endearments were over or there was a pause in them, Charles would lean back in his chair with a gusty sigh, arch his chest up, stretch out his legs and say: 'Well, come on. Tell me about the family.'

Then she would have to tell him about the White House. Her cheeks burnt as she thought how it would all come out. There seemed no chance yet of Agatha or Maisie getting married. That was what Charles would want to know chiefly about his sisters. He had a whole-some contempt for virginity. He would want to know how Doris, whom he rather admired, was 'coming along'. Those sisters of Charles's always sounded rather dreadful young women, not the sort that Agatha, Maisie or Doris would care to know. It seemed to Charles funny – he often referred to it – that Agatha wanted babies so badly and went all tender and conscious when babies were mentioned.

'She'll make no end of a fuss over our kids,' Charles would say. The White House seemed to Charles, all the same, very proper as an institution; it was equally proper that he should have a contempt for it. He helped to support the girls and his mother, for one thing, and that did place them all at a disadvantage. But they were dear, good souls – Mrs. Charles knelt with her hands on her knees and the hands clenched slowly from anger and helplessness.

Mrs. Ray, the mother of Charles, suddenly knelt down by his wife and put an arm round her shoulders without saying a word. She did these impulsive things grace-fully. Mrs. Charles relaxed and leant sideways a little against the kind shoulder. She had nothing to say, so they watched the fire struggle and heard the hall clock counting away the seconds.

'Have you got enough clothes on?' said Mother after a minute. 'It's cold in trains. I never do think you wear enough clothes.'

Mrs. Charles, nodding, unbuttoned her coat and

showed a ribbed sweater pulled on over her jumper. 'Sensible of me!' she proudly remarked.

'You're learning to be quite a sensible little thing,' Mother said lightly. 'I expect Charles will notice a difference. Tell Charles not to let you go out in the damp in your evening shoes. But I expect he knows how to take care of you.'

'Indeed, yes,' said Mrs. Charles, nodding.

'You're precious, you see.' Mother smoothed back the hair from against Mrs. Charles's cheek to look at her thoughtfully, like a gentle sceptic at some kind of miracle. 'Remember to write me about the flat: I want to know everything: wallpapers, views from the windows, sizes of rooms—— We'll be thinking about you both tomorrow.'

'I'll be thinking of you.'

'Oh, no, you won't,' said Mother, with perfect finality.

'Perhaps not,' Mrs. Charles quickly amended.

Mother's son Charles was generous, sensitive, gallant and shrewd. The things he said, the things he had made, his imprint, were all over the White House. Sometimes he looked out at Louise with bright eyes from the family talk, so striking, so unfamiliar that she fell in love with the stranger for moments together as a married woman should not. He was quiet and never said very much, but he *noticed*; he had an infallible understanding and entered deeply, it seemed, into the sisters' lives. He was so good; he was so keen for them all to be happy. He had the strangest way of anticipating one's wishes. He was master of an inimitable drollery – to hear him chaff Agatha! Altogether he was a knightly person, transcending modern convention. His little wife had come to them all in a glow from her wonderful lover. No wonder she was so quiet; they used to try and read him from her secret, sensitive face.

A thought of their Charles without his Louise troubled them all with a pang when Louise was her dearest. Charles in Lyons uncomplaining, lonely, tramping the town after business to look for a flat. The return of Louise to him, to the home he had found for her, her room upstairs already aghast and vacant, the emptiness that hung over them, gave them the sense of pouring out an oblation. The girls were heavy, with the faces of Flemish Madonnas; Doris achieved some resemblance to Charles, but without being handsome. They had cheerful dispositions, but were humble when they considered themselves; they thought Louise must have a great deal of love in her to give them so much when there was a Charles in her life.

Mrs. Ray, with a groan at her 'old stiff bones', got up from the hearthrug and sat on a chair. She thought of something to say, but was not quite ready to say it till she had taken up her knitting. She had hoped to have finished this pair of socks in time to send out by Louise with his others: she hadn't been able to – Mrs. Ray sighed. 'You're making my boy very happy,' she said, with signs in her manner of the difficulty one has in expressing these things.

Louise thought: 'Oh, I love you!' There was something about the hands, the hair, the expression, the general being of Mother that possessed her entirely, that she did not think she could live without. She knelt staring at Mother, all in a tumult. Why be so lonely, why never escape? She was too lonely, it couldn't be borne; not even for the sake of the White House. Not this morning, so early, with the buffeting strangeness of travel before her, with her wrists so chilly and the anticipation of sea-sickness making her stomach ache. The incommunicableness of even these things, these little ills of the body, bore Mrs. Charles down. She was tired of being brave alone, she was going to give it up.

It is with mothers that understanding and comfort are found. She wanted to put down her head on a bosom, this bosom, and say: 'I'm unhappy. Oh, help me! I can't go on. I don't love my husband. It's death to be with him. He's grand, but he's rotten all through——' She needed to be fortified.

'Mother——' said Louise.

'Mm-mm?'

'If things were not a success out there—— If one weren't a good wife always——' Mother smoothed her knitting out and began to laugh; an impassable, resolute chuckle.

'What a *thing*——' she said. 'What an idea!'

Louise heard steps in the hall and began kneading her hands together, pulling the fingers helplessly. '*Mother*,' she said, 'I feel——'

Mother looked at her; out of the eyes looked Charles. The steady, gentle look, their interchange, lasted moments. Steps came hurrying over the flags of the hall.

'I can't go——'

Doris came in with the teapot. She wasn't grown up, her movements were clumsy and powerful, more like a boy's. She should have been Charles. Her heavy plait came tumbling over her shoulder as she bent to put down the teapot – round and brown with a bluish glaze on it. Sleep and tears in the dark had puffed up her eyelids, which seemed to open with difficulty: her small eyes dwindled into her face. '*Breakfast*,' she said plaintively.

Rose, the servant, brought in a plate of boiled eggs – nice and light for the journey – and put them down compassionately.

'Even Rose,' thought Mrs. Charles, getting up and coming to the table obediently because they all expected her to, 'even Rose——' She looked at the breakfast-cups with poppies scattered across them as though she had not seen them before or were learning an inventory. Doris had begun to eat as though nothing else mattered. She took no notice of Louise, pretending, perhaps, to make things easier for herself, that Louise were already gone.

'Oh, Doris, not the *tussore* tie with the *red* shirt.' Whatever White House might teach Mrs. Charles about common sense, it was her mission to teach them about clothes. 'Not,' said Mrs. Charles, with bravado rising to an exaggeration of pathos, 'not on my last day!'

'I dressed in the dark; I couldn't see properly,' said Doris.

'You won't get eggs for breakfast in France,' said Maisie with a certain amount of triumph as she came in and sat down.

'I wonder what the flat'll be like?' said Maisie. 'Do write and tell us about the flat – describe the wallpapers and everything.'

'Just think,' said Doris, 'of Charles buying the furniture! "*Donnez-moi une chaise!*" "*Bien, Monsieur.*" "*Non. Ce n'est pas assez comfortable pour ma femme.*" '

'Fancy!' said Maisie, laughing very much. 'And fancy if the flat's high up.'

'There'll be central-heating and stoves. Beautiful fug.

She actually won't be chilly.' Mrs. Charles was always chilly: this was a household joke.

'Central heating is stuffy——'

Doris broke away suddenly from the conversation. 'Oh!' she said violently, 'Oh, Louise, you are *lucky*!'

A glow on streets and on the pale, tall houses: Louise walking with Charles. Frenchmen running in blousey overalls (Doris saw), French poodles, French girls in plaid skirts putting the shutters back, French ladies on iron balconies, leaning over, watching Charles go up the street with Louise and help Louise over the crossings; Charles and Louise together. A door, a lift, a flat, a room, a kiss! 'Charles, Charles, you are so splendid! Mother loves you and the girls love you and I love you——' 'Little woman!' A French curtain fluttering in the high, fresh wind, the city under the roofs – forgotten. All this Doris watched: Louise watched Doris.

'Yes,' smiled Louise. 'I *am* lucky.'

'Even to be going to France,' said Doris, and stared with her dog's eyes.

Louise wanted to take France in her two hands and make her a present of it. 'You'll be coming out soon, Doris, some day.' (It was not likely that Charles would have her – and did one, anyhow, dare let the White House into the flat?)

'Do you really think so?'

'Why not, if Mother can spare you?'

'*Louise!*' cried Maisie reproachfully – she had been sitting watching – 'you aren't eating!'

Agatha, sitting next her, covered up her confusion with gentle, comforting noises, cut the top off an egg and advanced it coaxingly. That was the way one made a child eat; she was waiting to do the same for Charles's and Louise's baby when it was old enough. Louise now almost saw the baby sitting up between them, but it was nothing to do with her.

'You'll be home in *less* than the two years, I shouldn't be surprised,' said Mother startlingly. It was strange, now one came to think of it, that any question of coming back to the White House had not been brought up before. They might know Mrs. Charles would be coming back, but they did not (she felt) believe it. So she smiled at Mother as though they were playing a game.

'Well, two years at the very least,' Mother said with energy.

They all cast their minds forward. Louise saw herself in the strong pale light of the future walking up to the White House and (for some reason) ringing the bell like a stranger. She stood ringing and ringing and nobody answered or even looked out of a window. She began to feel that she had failed them somehow, that something was missing. Of course it was. When Louise came back next time she must bring them a baby. Directly she saw herself coming up the steps with a child in her arms she knew at once what was wanted. Wouldn't Agatha be delighted? Wouldn't Maisie 'run on'? Wouldn't Doris hang awkwardly round and make jokes, poking her big finger now and then between the baby's curling pink ones? As for Mother – at the supreme moment of handing the baby to Mother, Louise had a spasm of horror and nearly dropped it. For the first time she looked at the baby's face and saw it was Charles's.

'It would do no *good*,' thought Mrs. Charles, cold all of a sudden and hardened against them all, 'to have a baby of Charles's.'

They all sat looking not quite at each other, not quite at her. Maisie said (thinking perhaps of the love-affair that never completely materialized): 'A great deal can happen in two years,' and began to laugh confusedly in an emotional kind of way. Mother and Agatha looked across at each other. 'Louise, don't forget to send us a wire,' said Mother, as though she had been wondering all this time she had sat so quiet behind the teapot whether Louise would remember to do this.

'Or Charles might send the wire.'

'Yes,' said Louise, 'that would be better.'

Polyphemus, knowing his moment, sprang up on to Mrs. Charles's knee. His black tail, stretched out over the tablecloth, lashed sideways, knocking the knives and forks crooked. His one green eye sardonically penetrated her. *He* knew. He had been given to Charles as a dear little kitten. He pressed against her, treading her lap methodically and mewing soundlessly, showing the purple roof of his mouth. 'Ask Charles,' suggested Polyphemus, 'what became of my other eye.' 'I know,' returned Mrs. Charles silently. '*They* don't, they haven't been told; you've a voice, I haven't – what about it?' 'Satan!' breathed Mrs. Charles, and caressed fascinatedly the fur just over his nose.

'Funny,' mused Agatha, watching, 'you never have cared for Polyphemus, and yet he likes you. He's a very transparent cat; he is wonderfully honest.'

'He connects her with Charles,' said Maisie also enjoying this interchange between the wife and the cat. 'He's sending some kind of a message – he's awfully clever.'

'Too clever for me,' said Mrs. Charles, and swept Polyphemus off her knee with finality. Agatha was going as far as the station; she went upstairs for her hat and coat. Mrs. Charles rose also, picked up her soft felt hat from a chair and pulled it on numbly, in front of the long glass, arranging two little bits of hair at the sides against her cheeks. 'Either I am dreaming,' she thought, 'or someone is dreaming me.'

Doris roamed round the room and came up to her. 'A book left behind, Louise; *Framley Parsonage,* one of your books.'

'Keep it for me.'

'For two years – all that time?'

'Yes, I'd like you to.'

Doris sat down on the floor and began to read *Framley Parsonage.* She went into it deeply – she had to go somewhere; there was nothing to say; she was suddenly shy of Louise again as she had been at first, as though they had never known each other – perhaps they never had.

'Haven't you read it before?'

'No, never, I'll write and tell you, shall I, what I think of it?'

'I've quite forgotten what *I* think of it,' said Louise, standing above her, laughing and pulling on her gloves. She laughed as though she were at a party, moving easily now under the smooth compulsion of Somebody's dreaming mind. Agatha had come in quietly. 'Hush!' she said in a strained way to both of them, standing beside the window in hat and coat as though *she* were the traveller. 'Hush!' She was listening for the taxi. Mother and Maisie had gone.

Wouldn't the taxi come, perhaps? What if it never came? An intolerable jar for Louise, to be deprived of going; a tear in the mesh of the dream that she could not endure. 'Make the taxi come soon!' she thought, praying now for departure. 'Make it come soon!'

Being listened for with such concentration must have frightened the taxi, for it didn't declare itself; there was not a sound to be heard on the road. If it were not for the hospitality of *Framley Parsonage* where, at this moment, would Doris have been? She bent to the pages absorbedly and did not look up; the leaves of the book were thin and turned over noisily. Louise fled from the morning-room into the hall.

Out in the dark hall Mother was bending over the pile of boxes, reading and re-reading the labels upside down and from all aspects. She often said that labels could not be printed clearly enough. As Louise hurried past she stood up, reached out an arm and caught hold of her. Only a little light came down from the staircase window; they could hardly see each other. They stood like two figures in a picture, without understanding, created to face one another.

'Louise,' whispered Mother, 'if things should be difficult—— Marriage isn't easy. If you should be disappointed — I know, I feel — you do understand? If Charles——'

'Charles?'

'I do love you, I do. You would tell me?'

But Louise, kissing her coldly and gently, said: 'Yes, I know. But there isn't really, Mother, anything to tell.'

THE JUNGLE

TOWARDS the end of a summer term Rachel
discovered the Jungle. You got over the wall at
the bottom of the kitchen garden, where it began
to be out of bounds, and waded through knee-high
sorrel, nettles and dock, along the boundary hedge of
Mr. Morden's property till you came to a gap in the
roots of the hedge, very low down, where it was possible
to crawl under. Then you doubled across his paddock
(this was the most exciting part), round the pond and
climbed a high board gate it was impossible to see through
into a deep lane. You got out of the lane farther down by
a bank with a hedge at the top (a very 'mangy' thin
hedge), and along the back of this hedge, able to
be entered at several points, was the Jungle. It was
full of secret dog-paths threading between enormous
tussocks of bramble, underneath the brambles there were
hollow places like caves; there were hawthorns one
could climb for a survey and, about the middle, a clump
of elders gave out a stuffy sweetish smell. It was an
absolutely neglected and wild place; nobody seemed to
own it, nobody came there but tramps. Tramps, whose
clothes seem to tear so much more easily than one's
own, had left little fluttering tags on the bushes, some
brownish newspaper one kicked away under the brambles,
a decayed old boot like a fungus and tins scarlet with

27

rust that tilted in every direction holding rain-water. Two or three of these tins, in some fit of terrible rage, had been bashed right in.

The first time Rachel came here, alone, she squeezed along the dog-paths with her heart in her mouth and a cold and horrible feeling she was going to find a dead cat. She knew cats crept away to die, and there was a sinister probability about these bushes. It was a silent July evening, an hour before supper. Rachel had brought a book, but she did not read; she sat down under the elders and clasped her hands round her knees. She had felt a funny lurch in her imagination as she entered the Jungle, everything in it tumbled together, then shook apart again, a little altered in their relations to each other, a little changed.

At this time Rachel was fourteen; she had no best friend at the moment, there was an interim. She suffered sometimes from a constrained, bursting feeling at having to keep things so much to herself, yet when she compared critically the girls who had been her great friends with the girls who might be her great friends she couldn't help seeing that they were very much alike. None of them any more than the others would be likely to understand . . . The Jungle gave her a strong feeling that here might have been the Perfect Person, and yet the Perfect Person would spoil it. She wanted it to be a thing in itself: she sat quite still and stared at the impenetrable bramble-humps.

On the last day of term Rachel travelled up in the train with a girl in a lower form called Elise Lamartine, who was going to spend the holidays riding in the New Forest. Elise had her hair cut short like a boy's and was supposed to be fearfully good at French but otherwise stupid. She had a definite quick way of doing things and a thoughtful slow way of looking at you when they were done. Rachel found herself wishing it weren't the holidays. She said, off-hand, as she scrambled down from the carriage into a crowd of mothers: 'Let's write to each other, shall we?' and Elise, beautifully unembarrassed, said, 'Right-o, let's!'

During the holidays Rachel became fifteen. Her mother let down her skirts two inches, said she really wasn't a little girl any more now and asked her to think about her career. She was asked out to tennis parties where strange young men had a hesitation about calling her anything and finally called her Miss Ritchie. Her married sister Adela promised that next summer holidays she'd have her to stay and take her to 'boy and girl dances'. 'Aren't I a girl now?' asked Rachel diffidently. 'You oughtn't to be a girl in that way till you're sixteen,' said Adela firmly.

Rachel had one terrible dream about the Jungle and woke up shivering. It was something to do with a dead body, a girl's arm coming out from under the bushes. She tried to put the Jungle out of her mind; she never thought of it, but a few nights afterwards she was back there again, this time with some shadowy person always a little behind her who turned out to be Elise. When they came to the bush which in the first dream had covered the arm she was trying to tell Elise about it, to make sure it *had* been a dream, then stopped, because she knew she had committed that murder herself. She wanted to run away, but Elise came up beside her and took her arm with a great deal of affection. Rachel woke up in a gush of feeling, one of those obstinate dream-taps that won't be turned off, that swamp one's whole

morning, sometimes one's day. She found a letter from
Elise on the breakfast-table.

Elise wrote a terrible letter, full of horses and brothers.
So much that might have been felt about the New
Forest did not seem to have occurred to her. Rachel was
more than discouraged, she felt blank about next term.
It was impossible to have a feeling for anyone who did
so much and thought nothing. She slipped the letter
under her plate and didn't intend to answer it, but later
on she went upstairs and wrote Elise a letter about
tennis parties. 'There has been talk,' she wrote, 'of my
going to boy and girl dances, but I do not feel keen on
them yet.'

'Who is your great friend now?' asked Mother, who
had come in and found her writing. She put on an
anxious expression whenever she spoke like this, because
Rachel was a Growing Daughter.

'Oh, no one,' said Rachel. 'I'm just dashing off something to one of the girls.'

'There was Charity. What about Charity? Don't you
ever write to her now?'

'Oh, I like her all right,' said Rachel, who had a
strong sense of propriety in these matters. 'I just think
she's a bit affected.' While she spoke she was wondering
whether Elise would get her remove or not. Rachel was
going up into IVa. It would be impossible to know anybody two forms below.

Next term, when they all came back, she found Elise
had arrived in IVb (one supposed on the strength of her
French), but she was being tried for the Gym Eight and
spent most of her spare time practising for it. Rachel
looked in at the Gym door once or twice and saw her
doing things on the apparatus. When she wasn't doing

things on the apparatus Elise went about with the same
rather dull girl, Joyce Fellows, she'd been going about
with last term. They sat together and walked together
and wrestled in the boot-room on Saturday afternoons.
Whenever Rachel saw Elise looking at her or coming
towards her she would look in the other direction or
walk away. She realized how the holidays had been
drained away by imagination, she had scarcely lived
them; they had been wasted. She had a useless, hopeless
dull feeling and believed herself to be homesick. By the
end of the first fortnight of term she and Elise had
scarcely spoken. She had not been back again to the
Jungle, of whose very existence she somehow felt
ashamed.

One Sunday, between breakfast and chapel, they
brushed against each other going out through a door.

'Hullo!' said Elise.

'Oh – hullo!'

'Coming out?'

'Oh – right-o,' said Rachel, indifferent.

'Anywhere special? I know of a tree with three
apples they've forgotten to pick. We might go round that
way and just see——'

'Yes, we might,' agreed Rachel. They went arm in
arm.

It was early October, the day smelt of potting-sheds
and scaly wet tree-trunks. They had woken to find a
mist like a sea round the house; now that was being
drawn up and the sun came wavering through it. The
white garden-gate was pale gold and the leaves of the
hedges twinkled. The mist was still clinging in sticky
shreds, cobwebs, to the box-hedges, the yellow leaves on
the espaliers, the lolling staggering clumps of Michael-

mas daisies; like shreds of rag, Rachel thought, clinging to brambles.

Elise's apple tree was half way down the kitchen-garden. They looked up: one of the apples was missing. Either it had fallen or some interfering idiot had succeeded in getting it down with a stone. The two others, beautifully bronze, nestled snugly into a clump of leaves about eight feet up. The girls looked round; the kitchen garden was empty.

'One could chuck things at them,' said Rachel, 'if one didn't make too much row.'

'I bet I could swing myself up,' said Elise confidently. She stepped back, took a short run; jumped and gripped a branch overhead. She began to swing with her legs together, kicking the air with her toes. Every time she went higher; soon she would get her legs over that other branch, sit there, scramble up into standing position and be able to reach the apples.

'How gymnastic we are!' said Rachel with the sarcastic admiration which was *de rigeur*. Elise half-laughed, she hadn't a breath to spare. She stuck out her underlip, measured the branch with her eye. Her Sunday frock flew back in a wisp from her waist; she wore tight black stockinette bloomers.

' – *Elise*' shrieked a voice from the gate. 'Rachel *Ritchie*! Leave that tree alone – what are you doing?'

'Nothing, Miss Smyke,' shouted Rachel, aggrieved.

'Well, don't,' said the voice, mollified. 'And don't potter! Chapel's in forty minutes – don't get your feet wet.'

Elise had stopped swinging, she hung rigid a moment, then dropped with bent knees apart. 'Damn!' she said naturally. Rachel said 'dash' herself, sometimes 'confound'. She knew people who said 'confound' quite often, but she had never had a friend of her own who said 'Damn' before. 'Don't be profane,' she said, laughing excitedly.

Elise stood ruefully brushing the moss from her hands. 'Damn's not profane,' she said. 'I mean, it's nothing to do with God.' She took Rachel's arm again, they strolled towards the end of the kitchen garden. 'Are you getting confirmed next term?'

'I think I am. Are you?'

'I suppose I am. Religion's very much *in* our family, you see. We were Huguenots.'

'Oh, I always wondered. Is that why you're called——'

'– Elise? Yes, it's in our family. Don't you like it?'

'Oh, I *like* it . . . But I don't think it suits you. It's such a silky delicate kind of a girlish name. You, you're too——' She broke off; there were people you couldn't talk to about themselves without a confused, excited, rather flustered feeling. Some personalities felt so much more personal. 'You ought to have some rather quick hard name. Jean or Pamela . . . or perhaps Margaret – *not* Marguerite.'

Elise was not listening. 'I ought to have been a boy,' she said in a matter-of-fact, convinced voice. She rolled a sleeve back. 'Feel my muscle! Watch it – look!'

'I say, Elise. I know of a rather queer place. It's near here, I discovered it. I call it the Jungle, just to distinguish it from other places. I don't mean it's a bit exciting or anything,' she said rapidly, 'it's probably rather dirty; tramps come there. But it is rather what I used to call "secret".' She was kicking a potato down the path before her, and she laughed as she spoke. Lately she had avoided the word 'secret'. Once, at the end of a visit, she had shown a friend called Charity a 'secret place' in their garden at home, and Charity had laughed to the others about it when they were all back at school.

'Which way?'

'Over the wall – you don't mind getting your legs stung?'

The nettles and docks were rank-smelling and heavy with dew. One was hampered by Sunday clothes; they tucked their skirts inside their bloomers and waded through. 'It's a good thing,' said Rachel, 'we've got black stockings that don't show the wet. Brown are the limit, people can see a high-water mark.' The wet grass in Mr. Morden's paddock squashed and twanged, it clung like wet snakes as they ran, cutting their ankles. She pulled up panting in the lane below. 'Sure you're keen?' said Rachel. 'There may be blackberries.'

When they came to the Jungle she pushed in ahead of Elise, parting the brambles recklessly. She didn't mind now if she *did* find a dead cat: it would be almost a relief. She didn't look round to see what Elise was doing or seemed to be thinking. They were down in a hollow, it was mistier here and an early morning silence remained. A robin darted out of a bush ahead of her. It was an even better place than she had remembered; she wished she had come here alone. It was silly to mix up people and thoughts. Here was the place where the dead girl's arm, blue-white, had come out from under the bushes. Here was the place where Elise, in the later dream, had come up and touched her so queerly. Here were the rags of her first visit still clinging, blacker and limper . . . the same boot——

'Like a nice boot?' she said facetiously.

Elise came up behind her, noisily kicking at one of the

tins. 'This is an awfully good place,' she said. 'Wish *I'd* found it.'

'It isn't half bad,' said Rachel, looking about her casually.

'Do you like this sort of thing – coming here?'

'I bring a book,' said Rachel defensively.

'Oh, that would spoil it. I should come here and make camp fires. I should like to come here and go to sleep. Let's come here together one Saturday and do both.'

'I think sleeping's dull,' said Rachel, surprised.

'I love it,' exclaimed Elise, hugging herself luxuriously. 'I can go to sleep like a dog. If wet wouldn't show too much on the back of my dress I'd lie down and go to sleep here now.'

'My dear – how *extraordinary*!'

'Is it?' said Elise, indifferent. 'Then I suppose I'm an extraordinary person.' She had stopped in front of a bush; there were a few blackberries, not very good ones; just like a compact, thick boy in her black tights she was sprawling over the great pouffe of brambles, standing on one foot, balancing herself with the other, reaching out in all directions. But for that way she had of sometimes looking towards one, blank with an inside thoughtfulness, one couldn't believe she had a life of her own apart from her arms and legs. Rachel angrily doubted it; she crouched beside the bush and began eating ripe and unripe blackberries indiscriminately and quickly. 'I am a very ordinary person,' she said aggressively, to see what would come of it. She wondered if Elise had a notion what she was really like.

'No, you're not,' said Elise, 'you're probably clever. How old are you?'

'I was fifteen in August. How old——'

'I shall be fifteen in March. Still, it's awful to think you're a whole form cleverer than I am.'

'I'm not clever,' said Rachel quickly.

Elise laughed. 'One queer thing,' she said, 'about being clever is that clever people are ashamed of it . . . Look what worms some of these brains here are – I say, if I eat any more of them I shall be sick. They're not a bit nice really, they're all seed, but I never can help eating things, can you?'

'Never,' said Rachel. 'At home I often used to eat three helpings – I mean of things like eclairs or pheasant or treacle tart – our cook makes it awfully well. I don't now that I have started staying up to late dinner. That makes an awful difference to what one eats in a day, helpings apart.'

'I'd never eat three helpings because of my muscles. I mean to keep awfully strong, not get flabby like women do. I know all the things men don't eat when they're in training. Do you?'

'No. Do you stay up to late dinner?'

'We don't have late dinner,' said Elise scornfully. 'We have supper and I've stayed up to that ever since I was eight.'

Elise's people must be very eccentric.

They were seen coming breathless across the garden twenty minutes late for chapel and found Miss Smyke at the door with a flaming sword. 'What did I say?' asked Miss Smyke, rhetorical. 'What did I *tell* you? It's no use going into chapel now,' she said spitefully (as though they would want to). 'They're at the Te Deum.

Go up and change your stockings and stay in your dormi-
tories till you're sent for.' She turned and went back
into chapel, looking satisfied and religious.

Being punished together was intimate; they felt
welded. They were punished more severely than usual
because of Elise, who had a certain way with her underlip . . . She had a way with her head, too, that reminded
Rachel of a defiant heroic person about to be shot. It
didn't come out, mercifully, that they had broken bounds;
the Jungle remained unmenaced. They were ordered
apart for the rest of the day (which sealed them as 'great
friends') and Rachel, usually humiliated by punish-
ment, went about feeling clever and daring. On Monday
evening she kept a place beside her for Elise at supper,
but after some time saw Elise come in arm in arm with
Joyce Fellows and sit down at another table. She looked
away. After supper Elise said, 'I say, why didn't you
come? Joyce and I were keeping a place for you.'

Term went on, and it was all rather difficult and
interesting. Rachel was a snob; she liked her friends to
be rather distinguished, she didn't like being 'ordered
about' by a girl in a lower form. That was what it
amounted to; Elise never took much trouble about one,
her down-right manner was peremptory: when she said,
'Let's——' it meant (and sounded like), 'You can if you
like: *I'm* going to.' Whenever they did things together
it ended in trouble; Rachel began to wish Elise wouldn't
stick out her lip at people like Casabianca and look down
her nose. Mistresses spoke scornfully about 'Going about
with the younger ones'. They never asked her to
'influence' Elise, which showed that they knew. IVB
seemed a long way down the school, yet Elise would
swagger ahead of one along passages and throw back,

without even looking: 'Buck up: do come on!' Then there was Joyce Fellows; a silly, blank-faced, rather unhappy 'entourage'.

One evening in prep Charity did a drawing on a page of her notebook, tore it out and passed it across to Rachel. It was called 'Jacob (Rachel's Rajah)', and was a picture of Elise in trousers hanging upside down from a beam in the gym roof and saying, in a balloon from her mouth, 'Buck up, come here, I'm waiting.' Rachel couldn't climb ropes and hadn't a good head when she did get to the top of things, so this was unkind. The name was stupid but the drawing was rather clever. Rachel showed it to Elise at supper and Elise turned scarlet and said, 'What a darned silly fool!' She hadn't much sense of humour about herself.

The next evening there was a drawing of a figure like two tennis balls lying on Charity's desk. (Charity's figure was beginning to develop feminine curves at an alarming rate.) Charity looked, laughed and picked the drawing up with the very tips of her finger and thumb. 'Of course I don't *mind* this,' she said, 'but I suppose you know your beastly little common friend has no business in our form-room?'

Rachel's cheeks burnt. It wouldn't have mattered a bit if the drawing had been clever, but Elise couldn't draw for toffee: it was just silly and vulgar. 'I don't know why you should think it was you,' she said, 'but if the cap fits——'

Later she rounded on Elise. 'If you did want to score off Charity you might have invented a cleverer way.'

'*I* don't pretend to be clever,' said Elise.

'I'd never have shown you the Jacob one if I'd thought

you were going to be such a silly serious ass,' stormed Rachel.

Elise stared with her wide-open pale grey eyes that had, this moment, something alert behind them that wasn't her brain. 'You knew that wouldn't be my idea of a funny joke,' she said, 'didn't you?'

Rachel hesitated. Elise, with tight lips, made a scornful little laughing sound in her nose.

'As a matter of fact,' said Rachel, 'I didn't think it mattered showing you what all my friends in my form think. You know you have got into a fearfully bossy way with everybody.'

'I don't know what you're talking about,' said Elise. 'I don't s'pose you do either. What do you mean by "everybody"? I never take any notice of anybody unless I happen to like them, and if they think I'm bossy I can't help it. It's not me who's bossy, but other people who are sloppy?'

'Do you think I'm sloppy?'

'Yes, you are rather sloppy sometimes.'

It was at supper, a dreadful place to begin a conversation of this sort. Rachel and Elise had to remain side by side, staring at the plates of the girls opposite, biting off and slowly masticating large mouthfuls of bread-and-jam. Then Rachel half-choked over a mouthful, turned away quickly and flung herself into the conversation of two girls on the other side. They all three talked 'shop' about algebra prep. Elise just sat on there, perfectly natural and disconcertingly close. When Rachel peeped round she did not notice. She sat badly, as always, her head hunched forward between her shoulders, and Rachel knew her lip was out and had a feeling that she was smiling. When grace was over they pushed back

their chairs and bolted out in different directions. Out
in the hall everybody was crowding up to the notice-
board. Rachel turned away and went into the class-
room and sat at her desk. When the others had gone she
came out and looked at the notice-board. The lists for
the next match were up and Elise was in the Lacrosse
Eleven.

The last Sunday but one, in the afternoon, Rachel
went back to the Jungle. It was December, goldenly
fine; the trees were pink in the afternoon light, rooks
circled, grass was crisp in the shadows from last night's
frost. She had started out in an overcoat with a muffler
up to her nose and rabbit-skin gloves, but soon she
untwisted the muffler and stuffed the gloves into her
pocket. The lovely thin air seemed to have turned
warmer; her breath went lightly and clearly away
through it. The wall, the hedge, the gate of the paddock
gave her a bruised feeling.

She stumbled across the paddock, tripping up on the
long ends of her muffler, with her unbuttoned overcoat
flapping against her legs. 'It will be a good end to this
kind of a term,' she thought. 'If Mr. Morden catches
me.'

It really hadn't been much of a term. She hadn't
worked, she hadn't been a success at anything, she
hadn't made anyone like her. The others in IVA had
been nice to her since she 'came back', but they forgot
her unintentionally; they had got into the way of
doing things together in twos and threes since the beginning of term and she got left out – naturally. She felt
lonely, aimless, absolutely inferior; she tried a lot of
new ways of doing her hair, designed a black velvet dress

for herself and looked forward to going home. She brought names, Charity's and the other girls', rather unnaturally into her letters so that Mother shouldn't suspect she was being a failure. She felt so sick for Elise that she prayed to be hit by a ball on the head every time she went out to Lacrosse.

Elise had the most wonderfully natural way of not seeing one. She said 'Sorry' when she bumped into one in the passage, shared a hymn-book in chapel when they found themselves side by side, and when she caught up and passed one going out to the playing-field side-glanced indifferently as though one were one of the seniors. She had got her colours after her third match; no one under fifteen had ever got their colours before. All the important people were taking her up and talking about her. IVA agreed that they would not have minded, they'd have been glad, if she'd only been humble and nice to begin with and not such an absolutely complacent pig. They never talked about her in front of Rachel and Rachel never mentioned her.

Down in the lane there were deep ruts; she walked between them on crumbling ridges. A dog was barking somewhere at Mr. Morden's, snapping bits out of the silence, then letting it heal again. The bank to the Jungle was worn slippery; Rachel pulled herself up it from root to root. The Jungle was in shadow; the grass had fallen like uncombed hair into tufts and was lightly frosted. 'It's nice to come back,' said Rachel. 'I never was really *here* that last time, it's awfully nice to come back.' She bent down, parting the brambles; the leaves were purple and blackish; some rotting brown leaves drifted off at her touch.

Coming out from the brambles, an arm was stretched

over the path. 'Not, O God, in this lonely place,' said Rachel – 'let there not be a body!'

She was shaken by something regularly, put up a hand to her heart with the conscious theatrical movement of extreme fear and found it thumping. The hand lay a yard ahead of her – she could have taken three steps forward and stepped on it – the thumb bent, the red, square-tipped fingers curling on to the palm.

'Elise, is this you?' whispered Rachel. She waited, plucking leaves from the bramble, hearing the dog bark, then went round to where Elise was lying in a valley between the brambles.

Elise lay half on her side, leaning towards the arm that was flung out. Her knees were drawn up, her other arm flung back under her head which rested, cheek down, on a pile of dead leaves as on a pillow and was wrapped up in a muffler. The muffler was slipping away from her face like a cowl. Down in the sheltered air between the bushes she was flushed by sleep and by the warmth of the muffler. She was Elise, but quenched, wiped-away, different; her mouth – generally pressed out straight in a grudging smile – slackened into a pout; thick short lashes Rachel had never noticed spread out on her cheeks. Rachel had never looked full at her without having to pass like a guard her direct look; her face now seemed defenceless. Rachel stood looking down – the only beautiful thing about Elise was that cleft in her chin. She stood till her legs ached, then shifted her balance. A twig cracked; Elise opened her eyes and looked up.

'I told you I'd come here and sleep,' she said.

'Yes – isn't it fearfully cold?'

Elise poked up her head, looked round and lay back

42

again, stretching luxuriously. 'No,' she said, 'I feel
stuffyish. Have you just come?'

'Yes. I'm going away again.'

'Don't go.' Elise curled up her legs to make room in
the valley. 'Sit down.'

Rachel sat down.

'Funny thing your just coming here. Have you come
much?'

'No,' said Rachel, staring into the brambles intently
as though she were watching something that had a lair
inside them moving about.

'I brought Joyce Fellows once; we came in here to
smoke cigars. I hate smoking – Joyce was as sick as a
cat.'

'How *beastly*!'

'Oh, I don't suppose there's anything left now, we
covered it up. Anyhow, I shall never smoke much. It's
so bad for the wind.'

'Oh, by the way,' said Rachel, 'congratulations about
your colours.'

Elise, her hands clasped under her head, had been
lying looking at the sky. 'Thanks so much,' she said,
now looking at Rachel.

'Aren't we mad,' said Rachel uneasily, 'doing this in
December?'

'Why shouldn't we if we're warm enough? Rachel,
why shouldn't we? – Answer.'

'It'll be dark soon.'

'Oh, dark in your eye!' said Elise, 'there's plenty of
time . . . I say, Rachel, I tell you a thing we might
do——'

Rachel wound herself up in her muffler by way of a
protest. She had a funny feeling, a dancing-about of the

thoughts; she would do anything, anything. "Pends what,' she said guardedly.

'You could turn round and round till you're really comfy, then I could turn round and put my head on your knee, then I could go to sleep again. . . .'

The round cropped head like a boy's was resting on Rachel's knees. She felt all constrained and queer; comfort was out of the question. Elise laughed once or twice, drew her knees up higher, slipped a hand under her cheek where the frieze of the overcoat tickled it.

'All right?' said Rachel, leaning over her.

'Mm – *mmm*.'

The dog had stopped barking, the Jungle, settling down into silence, contracted a little round them, then stretched to a great deep ring of unrealness and loneliness. It was as if they were alone on a ship, drifting out. . . .

'Elise,' whispered Rachel, 'do you think we———'

But the head on her knees had grown heavy. Elise was asleep.

SHOES:

AN INTERNATIONAL EPISODE

THEIR room was in morning disorder. To keep
the french window open at its widest an armchair
smothered in clothes had been pushed up, a
curtain tied back with one of Mrs. Aherne's stockings.
She had stripped the beds – one could never be certain
hotel femmes-de-chambre did this thoroughly – and
two great scrolls of bedclothes toppled over the room like
baroque waves. The two had breakfasted; the coffee-
tray, lodged on a table-edge among brushes, collars and
maps, was littered with cigarette-ends, stained beet
sugar and crumbs of roll. Mr. Aherne did not care for
the crumby part and had an untidy habit of scooping this
out with his thumb.

Outside, the pale glare of morning, unreal like mid-
summer sunshine remembered at Christmas, painted
garden tree-tops, blonde tiled roofs, and polished some
green glass balls cemented on to a wall till one wanted
to reach out and touch them.

Mrs. Aherne, feeling French and sophisticated,
wandered round in her dressing-gown smoking a
cigarette. Her husband bowing forward into the looking-
glass carefully parted his hair. It was exquisite to be
leisurely. Her chemise, back from a French laundress,
was delicate on her skin.

'All the same,' she said, 'I wish you would hurry up with that glass. What about *my* hair?'

'You look lovely the way you are,' said Mr. Aherne, studying himself sympathetically.

She felt she did. She really was a pretty thing; blonde, brown, vigorous. She said:

'I should hate them to think all Englishwomen were frumpy.'

'You may be certain they don't. I saw two of them turn and have a good look at you going out of the dining-room——'

'Really? . . . Oh, don't be so silly!'

Mr. Aherne, in shirt-sleeves, looking like one of those nice advertisements of shaving-soap, dived out into the passage to bring in the shoes. He reappeared, put them down and looked at them with a smile. These two pairs of shoes, waiting outside for him every morning, still seemed a formal advertisement to the world of their married state. 'Nice little couple,' said Edward Aherne.

Dillie didn't notice the shoes at once; she, in possession of the looking-glass, was powdering over the sunburn at the base of her throat. But when she turned round she said sharply:

'Edward, what are *these* doing in here? They're not mine!'

The female shoes, uncertainly balanced because of their high heels, listed towards the strong shoes of Edward timidly and lackadaisically. They were fawn kid, very clean inside (so probably new), low at the insteps, with slim red heels and a pattern in scarlet leather across the strap and over the toe-cap. They were tiny (size three or three-and-a-half) and looked capable solely of an ineffectual, somehow alluring totter.

'These are *not* my shoes,' repeated Mrs. Aherne ominously.

Edward, incredulous, came to look at the shoes. His face went into stiff lines, conscious of being searched.

'*I* never——'

'I didn't suppose you did . . .' She flashed with anger. 'Oh, but what little horrors! How *could* they think——!'

'They didn't think; they got muddled up about rooms.'

'There was no mistake about *your* shoes.'

'I wonder,' said Edward archly, 'who yours have been spending the night with!'

Not feeling French any longer, she wasn't amused. She threw her cigarette out of the window – to smoke more than one after breakfast made her feel stuffy, anyhow.

Dillie was an advanced, intelligent girl who had married Edward two years ago. Since then they had travelled a good deal. She had been constant to the good resolutions made on her honeymoon: not to be insular, not to behave like a 'dear little thing'. She never grumbled at rich cooking, at having no egg for breakfast and no pudding; when Latins ogled she frowned in the other direction but did not complain to Edward. She tried to share Edward's elation when café waiters brought her *La Vie Parisienne*. 'They wouldn't bring *that* to most Englishwomen!' Edward used to exclaim: she wondered why they didn't bring it to Frenchwomen either. She walked about France in good brogues and didn't mind if her feet looked a shade powerful. She took six-and-a-halfs for ordinary wear and, when she wanted to be really comfortable, sevens.

To be annoyed by the simpering shoes was unworthy;

she said reasonably: 'Well, find mine, and put those wherever mine were.'

'Everyone else's have been taken in, I noticed; ours were the last.'

He was *too* helpless; she snorted. 'Then give them to me!'

The passage outside was stuffy and panelled with doors. Dillie paced up and down, swinging the shoes by their straps, raging. Those doors were cynical. She looked at the numbers each side of their own; No. 19 clicked open and a man with no collar looked out at her ardently, but with a shake of the head shut the door again in discouragement. Dillie bristled. She was now quite certain the horrors belonged to his wife, or at any rate (one couldn't blink at these things) to the lady in there with him. If he hadn't put the matters on such a basis she would have knocked and presented them. She jumped as door No. 11 opened behind her and a lady in red crêpe-de-chine came out on a gust of geranium powder.

'*Ceux sont à vous, peut-etre?*' said Dillie, advancing the shoes nervously and forgetting '*Madame*'. The lady said '*Merci*', and went by in repudiation, chillingly. The shoes were in no worse taste than her own and, at least, cleaner. Dillie, now on the defensive, returned to her room. 'Better ring, I suppose,' she said stormily.

The worst, at any crisis, of these jolly little hotels is that the *sommelier* is the waiter and disappears between ten and eleven, delegating upstairs business to the femme-de-chambre who is sympathetic but irrational. The femme-de-chambre, on appearance, was desolated for Madame but knew nothing. She dangled the horrors temptingly; they were '*des jolies chaussures . . . mig-nonnes*'.

'*Je ne pourrais pas même les porter. Aussi, je les
deteste. Enlevez-les.*'

The femme-de-chambre languished at Edward.

'*Enlevez-les,*' Edward said sternly. '*Et allez demander.
Les chaussures de Madame. . . .*'

'*C'est ça!*' agreed the femme-de-chambre, inspired.
She vanished and did not return.

Meanwhile it was half-past ten. 'We meant to have
done that *jubé* before lunch and if we do it now we won't
get back till one. By that time the *hors-d'œuvres* will have
been picked over and we shall get nothing but those
beastly little bits of sausage. How greedy the French are.
And I always did think this hotel was sinister. I told
you so at the time, Edward.'

'Oh, my darling. . . .'

'Well, not last night, but I had that cherry brandy
and there was the moon.'

They went out, finally, into the hardening brilliance.
Dillie, unwillingly elegant in snakeskins she'd been
keeping for the Americans in Carcassonne, tottered over
the *pavé*. Edward turned down his panama over his eyes
and assumed with his chin a subdued expression. It
really *was* annoying for Dillie. They went unseeingly
through the market: he offered Dillie peaches. 'How,'
she said scornfully, 'can we possibly eat peaches in a
cathedral?'

'Oh . . . we *are* going there?' said Edward deferentially.

'Well, we don't want to waste a morning absolutely,
I suppose. We will at least,' she said vindictively '*begin*
the *jubé*.'

As they turned down the Rue des Deux Croix towards
the cathedral bold in sunshine, somebody swept off a hat
ineffably. It was the collarless man with the expression,

now in a very low, tight collar over which his neck hung out voluptuously. Dillie wore one of the local hats of thin, limp, peach-coloured straw; Edward side-glanced vainly under the drooping brim. She did not speak; he said nothing.

The cathedral mounted over them, they blinked, incredulous, up at the façade. Lost to one other, they went silently into the pointed, chilly darkness.

After half an hour the back of Edward's neck was aching from much admiration; he said he would like a drink. Dillie, who had pinned back the flap of her hat, looked through him ethereally. She supposed men were like that. '*I'll* just sit here,' she said. 'Edward . . . ?'

'Dearest?'

'Has one got a terribly little soul? How could one have felt shoes mattered!'

He couldn't imagine, either. 'But you're sure,' he said respectfully, 'you wouldn't care for a *little* drink?'

She couldn't even bring the idea into focus, so he went out alone to the café. He thought how much more spiritual women were. But before his drink arrived she came limping across the square. She thought perhaps she had better have something to pick her up. 'You see, my feet are rather hurting. I can't – absorb. It's these high heels on the *pavé*.'

He ordered another mixed vermouth, and a syphon. 'Just think how you'd feel if you were wearing things like those . . . like the horrors.'

'Just think of wearing them always. Oh, Edward, what a conception of women!'

'What a conception!' echoed Edward with vehemence, looking round for the waiter. He laid a hand for a moment on the hand of his wife and companion, but she, relentlessly intelligent, slipped hers away. She was waiting for something, she had planned a discussion. The vermouths arrived; Edward looked at his wisely. 'Queer thing, life,' he said, marking time.

'Queer,' accepted Dillie. 'Of course they *were* pretty,' she said, and looked at him sideways.

'*I* thought so——' said Edward rashly.

'I knew you did! Why couldn't you say so? Oh, Edward, do I deserve that kind of thing? Can't you be frank? I could see that at once by the way you looked at them. You are so transparent. Why *can't* you be frank?'

'It seems rather waste to be frank if I'm transparent.'

'I suppose no men really want to respect women. Frenchmen are franker, that's all. What men really want——'

'My darling, I do wish you needn't generalize about "men".' She was ignoring her vermouth; he felt constrained to put down his glass.

'I do sometimes wonder how really modern you are.'

'Darling——'

'Don't keep on calling me "darling"; it's like being patted. Would I have come out all this way with you and be staying in this stuffy embarrassing dishonest hotel eating unwholesome food, miles from all my friends, if I were simply a little wifie?'

'I knew you really wanted to go to the seaside with the Phippses.'

This was too much. 'If I had wanted to go to the seaside with the Phippses I'd have gone. You know we believe in freedom.'

'Of course I know. I think we do nearly always mean the same thing, only sometimes one of us expresses it unhappily. I *did* think you liked the food here; you agreed that half the fun of a morning abroad was wondering what there would be for lunch.'

'There are no vitamines. The salads are so oily. However,' said Dillie, 'we needn't go on like this, need we, just outside the cathedral?' She had a nice sense of locality and was most particular as to where they quarrelled and where they made love. Smiling at him with a calculated amiability, she began sipping her vermouth.

At lunch, when they had finished with the *hors-d'œuvres*, Edward asked the waiter, who seemed to be influential, about Dillie's shoes. The waiter, surprised and interested, admitted someone must have deceived himself. It was curious.

'*C'est ennuyant pour Madame,*' Edward said accusingly.

Dillie said in an undertone: 'Can't you possibly think of anything stronger?' Edward frowned at her. '*Très ennuyant,*' he said with a Gallic gesticulation: Dillie guarded the wine-bottle. The waiter watched in surprise, as though it occurred to him that foreigners gesticulated a good deal. He would make inquiries; without doubt some lady had also deceived herself. Reassuringly, he swept away the *hors-d'œuvres*.

'*Quelque dame* couldn't possibly have *se trompèed,*' said Dillie, furious. 'Somebody in this hotel is definitely dishonest.'

'As a matter of fact,' Edward said, 'this *is* rather interesting. I had heard the best type of French were becoming increasingly Anglophile. Someone will send your brogues along certainly; they're probably back by now, but meanwhile, someone will have been taking note of them, to copy.' Any sign of a theory justifying itself gave Edward a happy, fulfilled feeling. He smiled: 'She will certainly get them copied.'

'Oh, do you really think so? Do you think p'raps it was one of those women who turned last night when I went out of the dining-room?'

Edward said he should not be at all surprised.

'O-oh . . . Then I do hope we haven't seemed unpleasant. I shouldn't like them to think one at all grudging. It *is* remarkable, isn't it, how we seem to be setting the tone. You know, I'm quite sure if brogue shoes came to be worn over here generally, there'd be quite a change in the Latin attitude towards women – I do wish you'd *listen*, Edward, and not keep looking furtively at the menu. If you want to read it, read it; I don't mind you being greedy so long as you're sincere about it.'

'I only wanted to see what was coming next – My darling, you know your husband lives to be sincere with you! – As a matter of fact, it's *vol-au-vent:* you like that, don't you? Now *do* go on about the Latin attitude. . . .'

They were lunching half out of doors, under a roof that covered part of the garden. Now and then, lizards flickered over the tiles at their feet. Just beyond, shadow came to an end with an edge like metal; there was a glare of gravel, palm trees leaned languid together, creeper poured flaming over a wall, and a row of young orange trees in bright glazed vases swaggered along a balustrade. Balanced in the hot stillness, the green glass balls on the wall-top snatched one's attention with their look of precariousness. At the garden's end, impermanent yellow buildings, fit to go down at a puff; intense and feverish, like a memory of Van Gogh's. A long cat,

53

slipping from vase to vase, fawned on its reflection in an unnatural ecstasy.

Dillie looked at all this, sideways. 'You do like this?' said Edward, anxious.

'If only it weren't so hot; I hate being hot after lunch. And the glare is so awful. Everything one looks at has – has an echo.'

'That's rather clever. I do wish you'd write, Dillie.'

Dillie liked being told she ought to write; she replied with complacency that she lacked the creative imagination. 'I'm afraid I'm too critical. I do wish one could be more imposed upon.'

'Yes, I do wish one could!'

'Oh, but *you* are,' said Dillie firmly. That disposed of Edward; she brushed some crumbs from under her elbows and settled down to explain why. They had coffee brought out, and liqueurs, and remained talking after the last of the other guests had stared and gone. They both felt they *analysed* better in France; and of course wine did intensify the personality. They discussed Edward and Dillie, Dillie in relation to Edward, Edward to Dillie, Edward and Dillie to Dillie's shoes, and Dillie's shoes to the Latin attitude. They discussed sex. They vaguely glowed at each other with admiration. The waiter hung round, flicking at empty tables; they saw him as a tree, dimly; they had no idea how aggravating they were. Clasped hands supporting their flushed faces, they looked mistily past the waiter.

When he broke into their circle of consciousness they were surprised. The shoes, he was more than delighted to say, had been traced. A lady had found them outside her door and taken them into her room in mistake for her own. She had returned them to No. 20; they awaited

Madame above. Dillie said 'There!' in triumph, got up and went out carefully between the tables. She had a pleasant feeling of extension, as though she were everywhere, on the table-tops, in the wine-bottles, in the waiter; wise with all of them. Every experience meant something; each had its place. She groped down the corridor, blind in the sudden darkness, singing.

Their room was still darker; the shutters were latched. Dillie kicked the snakeskin shoes off her aching feet, then let daylight in with a bang and a blast of hot air. She turned to look for her brogues.

Reflected, swan-like, into the waxy floor, the Horrors awaited her. Heel to heel, they radiated sex-consciousness; dangling their little scarlet straps. '*Les chaussures de Madame*' – shoes attributed to Dillie Aherne, the frank and equal companion of Edward. 'You *damned*!' said Dillie. 'You absolutely *damned* damned!' Then she picked them up (she could never explain what came to her) and threw them one by one out of the window, aiming very carefully at a particular point in the sky. One struck the dining-room roof and ricocheted off it. The other spun on the sky with a flash of bright heel and dropped into a palm tree. Dillie grinned fearfully after them; then, shocked unutterably, buried her face in the curtain. Tears came on; she was caught in them, helpless, as in a thunder-shower.

Edward and she were both interested in her temper and in a kind of way proud of it. It was an anachronism but rather distinctive. But it sometimes came on her unprepared and so frightened and really hurt her. 'Oh!' she cried, trembling, 'Oh oh *oh*!' The curtain tore.

At the sound of the shoe on the roof Edward ran out, looked down at the shoe and up at the window. He saw his Dillie back in the darkness, hiding her face in the curtain.

'A shoe's just come down . . . Oh?'

Dillie wound herself up in the curtain.

Edward swallowed. 'Shall – shall I come up?' he said loyally.

Dillie unwound, and leant out to give emphasis. 'You can tell them the other's up in a palm tree – it has as much business there as in my room. Tell them they're vilely cynical and that we shall be leaving tonight.' She slammed the shutter.

'Scene in the best French manner,' Edward admitted. Several other shutters opened an inch or two; he felt people looking out at him sympathetically. He hurried across to the foot of a likely palm: up there, sure enough, was the little siren, lodged at the base of two fronds. It looked as though a shake of the tree should bring it down easily: he tried two or three and they didn't. He walked round the tree, looking up; he bombarded the shoe with pebbles; it faintly wobbled. He eyed it, without prejudice . . . it *was* rather a nice little shoe. Perhaps it belonged to the girl in pleated green organdie, with the gazelle eyes . . . (An ultra-feminine type, Dillie and he had agreed.) It would look rather jolly with pleated green organdie . . . The scarlet straps would compete with the scarlet hat – under which the gazelle eyes looked out deprecatingly, mysteriously. He wondered what she would think of him, trying to rout her shoe out of a palm with a piece of bamboo – the bamboo was too short. He might have swarmed up the trunk, but that would look silly and ruin his trousers. When she appeared, he would say to that girl. . . .

He hoped Dillie wouldn't summon him. Her tempers,

once over the crying stage, were very explicit. Hypnotically, the sky glittered through the fronds; caressing one shoe, gazing up at the other, Edward remained in a dream.

Dillie sat on her bed in the smothering darkness, wondering what to do now. She thought that, to keep her word at its present high value with Edward, she should pull the suitcases out and begin packing. She sighed; she did hope Edward would rush in and over-persuade her before she had put in the first layer. 'It's nothing personal,' she repeated, 'it's just that I cannot tolerate cynical inefficiency. I'm sorry, Edward; I just happen to be made like that.' She felt that if she could not say this to somebody soon it would lose its first edge of conviction; she peeped through the shutters, but Edward was standing stupidly under a palm tree and *she* wasn't going to call him. Reluctantly, she rolled up two jumpers. It really was queer how men failed one; one looked to them at a crisis, and they just walked away and stood under a tree with their legs apart. She tossed some paper out of a suitcase, trying to think of the French for 'inefficiency'.

Somebody knocked. Dillie stood still a moment; her lips moved. She powdered her nose which, still flushed with anger, felt larger than usual, then opened the door fiercely. An arch little boy in a blouse, called Anatole, stood outside with her brogues. '*V'la les chaussures de Monsieur,*' said Anatole, putting them down briskly. And he had been sent, he said, to look for the shoes that Madame had taken this morning, that did not belong to Madame at all, that belonged to another lady who now searched for them everywhere. He looked at Dillie, severely.

Dillie faltered, *'Comment?'*

Anatole very politely shrugged. *'Mais voila les chaussures de Monsieur,'* he repeated, and held out her brogues encouragingly.

'– de Monsieur.' It was the moment, certainly, for Dillie to make a demonstration. *Now* she could show them. *'Ceux ne sont pas——'* began Dillie. But she went scarlet and stopped. *Was* Anatole worth it – so small, so sleek, already so irreclaimable? She looked down; her good brogues sat there stodgily, square on the parquet. There was no nonsense about them. *'Les chaussures de Monsieur. . . .'*

'Allez-vous-en!' snapped Dillie, and slammed the door.

Ten minutes later, felt hat pulled on jauntily, she clattered happily to and fro on the parquet, brogued once more to resume the day. She was loth to waste an hour. She must make Edward feel how he was forgiven. She parted the shutters and looked out; a curious group intrigued her.

Edward, crossing the garden, was followed by the waiter at one end of a ladder and Anatole at the other. A girl in green ruffles was supported in indignation by two men, one in a Homburg, one in a flat cap. She was just the sort of girl for the shoes, Dillie observed with triumph. Edward was pink; it was trying for him, but one must not be sentimental. The waiter propped the ladder against the palm and after some discussion began to go up it; Anatole held the bottom and Edward directed.

'Je ne sais pas comment c'est arrivé,' Edward kept explaining. *'À gauche, un peu plus à gauche! Là – secouez-le . . . Je ne sais pas comment c'est arrivé. Ca a l'air, n'est-ce pas, d'etre tombé! Oui, c'est tombé, sans doute.'*

It was painful, in fact, to listen to the lying of Edward. Dillie, hot to the very back-bone, turned from the window; she even shut the shutters defensively. She kept moving about the room, jerked her hat off and came to a full-stop in front of the glass. Her eyes in the half-dark were haggard and rather profound; she looked startled. She tried to see Edward's Dillie: her thoughts raced round and round till one half suspected, inside this whirlwind of thought, there was nothing at all! She remembered the two Ahernes, vis-à-vis, at happy lunch-time, analysing each other; she envied them now like strangers. Such assurance, such a *right* kind of self-sufficiency . . . Goaded, Dillie pulled her hat on again, seized her stick and made for the door – then, in a queer kind of panic, returned and stood waiting for something, someone. The travelling clock loudly, officiously ticked.

Edward at last came up. He rippled a tap and entered, ruefully smiling. He was still rather warm.

'Well!' said Dillie.

'Squared 'em all. Wasn't it like a French farce though – not the improper kind. See us?'

'Partly. That terrible girl with the hips. Aren't French women *hard*, Edward!'

'Oh no, she was wonderfully sporting. Once she got her shoe back, she seemed rather amused. After all, Dillie, allowing for tastes, one does value one's shoes. I liked the two men she was with, too; of course they began by being rather aggressive – the French have a strong sense of property – but they finished up quite sympathetic and nice. You know, I always think——'

' – Did they *guess?*'

They looked at each other a moment in naked dis-comfort. Edward blinked. '*I* don't know: didn't ask them. Of course, the shoes had been traced to our room. . . .'

'I dare say,' Dillie said, unconcerned, 'she thought you looked like the Prince of Wales. You do, in that suit.'

'Do I? Good!'

Dillie steeled herself. Edward *was* rather pathetic. If one had been a 'wee wifey' sort of a person one would have clung to his chest, stroked the back of his nice neck and dithered: 'Oh, Edward, I've been such a beast, such a fool!' Dillie was glad she wasn't going to do this: it would have lowered her in Edward's eyes. It would have been shocking to drop the thing to the emotional plane and let it remain there, unanalysed, undiscussed.

'Queer,' she said bravely, 'what one gains with these people by an apparent access of uncontrol . . . They'd admire hysterics – Don't you agree?' she said sharply.

Edward went to the basin and made a loud noise with the tap. He rubbed water up his face. He gurgled into the water.

'What *do* you think – really, Edward?'

'Can't think now – I'm too hot.'

'Edward, you *don't* think I——? Surely, Edward——'

'Coming out?' said Edward, looking round for his hat.

Dillie felt quite hollow. What was Edward thinking? How dare he! . . . 'Edward, kiss me . . . You *do* believe in me? *Edward!* Kiss me!'

But Edward still seemed bothered about his hat. She supposed this might well be the end of their marriage.

Then a kiss from Edward uncertainly placed, began to be prolonged with some ardour in the dark room.

'You poor little angel!'

'You know, I did throw them out of the window.'

'You take things too hard, darling.'

'You do see I was right?' she said anxiously. She heard Edward breathe hard, considering.

'Under these particular circumstances – yes, I'm sure you were.'

'You weren't ashamed of me?' She couldn't let go of his coat-sleeve till he had answered.

'It was awful for you.'

'It was just,' she said, 'that I *cannot* tolerate cynical inefficiency.'

'You were quite right . . . Shall we go out now and have a rather long, cool drink before we look at any more of the cathedral? Bière blonde or something . . . Coming?'

'Yes,' she said, 'if you really must.' With infinite patronage, infinite affection, she took his arm.

Mr. and Mrs. Aherne, free, frank on terms of perfect equality, clattered down the corridor, disturbing some dozen siestas. Talking loudly together about the Latin mentality, they passed with a blink and a gasp into the reeling glare of the afternoon.

THE DANCING-MISTRESS

ABOUT half-past three at the end of November a
sea-fog came up over the edge of the cliff and,
mounting the plate-glass windows, filled the
Metropole ballroom with premature twilight. The
fantastic trees in the garden sank in like a painting on
blotting-paper; the red roofs of surrounding houses
persisted an hour in ever-ghostlier violet and faded at
last. Below the gold ceiling the three chandeliers draped
in crystal flowered reluctantly into a thin batch of lights:
the empty floor of the ballroom was pointed with yellow
reflections.

The door of the ladies' cloak-room kept creaking and
swinging, gusts of chatter came out from the little girls
being unpeeled from their wraps. Inside was a shuffle
of feet on the muffling carpet, water gushing in basins, a
clatter of ivory brush-backs on marble slabs. The mothers
and governesses wanted elbow-room for their business
with combs, for the re-tying of sashes and tugging of
woolly gaiters from silk-clad legs. With their charges,
they overflowed into the corridor. Here, all along, it was
chilly and rustling with muslins; Shetlands and cardi-
gans were flung over the radiators; little girls sat in
rows on the floor to put on their dancing-sandals. Miss
James, the dancing-mistress, hurrying past in her fur
coat with her dispatch-case, with her frail forward slant
like a reed in the current, was obliged to pick her way

over their legs. This she did with stereotyped little weary amused exclamations: her pianist followed in silence, a sharper, more saturnine profile against the brocaded wallpaper.

Miss James and the pianist went into the ballroom, where they opened their dispatch-cases behind the piano and, holding the mirror for one another, dusted over their faces with large soft puffs. The pianist moistened the tips of her fingers to flatten her hair back; it was polished against her skull like a man's. Miss James took the mirror and, biting her lip, glanced once more at herself in the oval with a slanting, fleeting, troubled kind of reproach.

The pianist looked up at the chandeliers, then scornfully out at the mist. 'I'm so glad we've got back to artificial – it seems much more natural, I think. – I say *sure* you don't feel too rotten?'

'Not as rotten as all that, I suppose,' said Miss James, indifferent. She had taken two classes already today; before the second she had declared a headache.

Miss Joyce James had begun as a pupil of Madame Majowski's; she worked for her now. Six days a week she went all over the country giving lessons; in the mornings she got up early to perfect her dancing at Mme Majowski's studio. She had eight dancing dresses like clouds, in gradations of beauty, a black satin tunic for studio practice, and besides these and the fur coat to cover them nothing at all but a cloth coat-and-skirt that looked wrong in the country and shabby in town. She was twenty-one, pretty but brittle and wax-like from steam-heated air. All day long she was just an appearance, a rhythm; in studio or ballroom she expanded into delicate shapes like a Japanese 'mystery' flower dropped into water. Late at night, she stopped 'seeming' too tired to 'be'; too tired to eat or to speak; she would finish long journeys asleep with her head on the pianist's shoulder: her sister received her with Bovril and put her to bed. Her eyebrows tilted outwards like wings; over her delicate cheekbones looked out, slightly tilted, her dreamy and cold eyes in which personality never awakened.

Miss James and Miss Peel the pianist sat for some minutes more in the window-embrasure behind the piano, side to side in jaded intimacy like a couple of monkeys. There was a radiator beside them. Miss Peel, having shivered out of her coat, kept spreading out her hands to the radiator, chafing them gently together, then spreading them out again, drawing in a reserve of warmth through the hands for her whole body. Her thin shoulder-blades rippled the silk of her dress as she bent forward. Miss James kept her eyes on the door, watching the children in, vacantly counting. As each came in its name jumped back to her memory as though a ticket had clicked up over its head. Though her mind was blank of this party of children from Wednesday to Wednesday, she never hesitated or was confused between the Joans and Jeans, the Margerys or the Mollies.

The little girls swung themselves in through the glass doors in twos and threes and skidded over the floor. The mothers and governesses sat down in groups round the walls with a resigned look of un-expectation. Their murmuring made a fringe round the silence, they nodded across at each other. The ballroom was gaunt in the vague smoky daylight, like a large church.

Three minutes before the class was due to begin, the hotel secretary appeared in the doorway, looking towards the piano. Miss Peel was sorting her music; she paused for a moment. 'There's Lulu,' she murmured.

'I know,' said Miss James.

Lulu, Romano-Swiss, fervent and graceful, looked away from them guiltily, looked round the room officially, switched on a dozen more lights. Miss James picked up a valse and frowned at it. She sighed, she was so tired. Two more little girls squeezed in past the secretary's elbow. The door swung to with a sigh.

'He's gone,' said Miss Peel and went back to her music.

'I know,' said Miss James.

A quarter to four. They both glanced at their wrist-watches, sighed and admitted the hour. The dancing-mistress came round the piano, the pianist sat down in front of 'Marche Militaire', shook back a slave-bangle up either arm, and waited, her eyes on Miss James who stood at the top of the room and looked down steadily into a looking-glass at the bottom.

'Good afternoon!' she said, silvery. The little girls ran forward, shaking out their dresses. 'Fall in for the March! Grizelda leading ... Skirts out, right foot pointed ... GO! ... *Right*, left – right – right – right—— Heads *well* up – *that's* right! ... Skirt, Phyllis ... Toes, Jean! ... Oh, *toes*, Margery – Margery, what *are* you doing ... *to-o-o-es!*'

Miss Peel spanked out the 'Marche Militaire'. Grizelda, impeccable, head erect, face blank, toes pointed quiver-ingly, led the twenty-five twice round the room and up the centre. Then they divided, ones right, twos left, met again, came up in twos, in fours, and then spaced out for the exercises. That was that.

The five positions: they performed like compasses. First ... second ... third ... fourth ... fifth! For each a chord, a shock of sound tingling out into silence. The dancing-mistress kept them in the fifth position and melted down between the lines to look.

Margery Mannering never did anything right. Her week was darkened by these Wednesdays. She was perfectly certain Miss James hated her – Miss James did. She was an overdressed little girl who belonged to a grandmother. She had red sausage-curls tied up with lop-eared white bows and spectacles that misted over, blinding her, when she got hot. She stood crooked forward anxiously. A coldness fingered its way down her spine as Miss James came softly to her down the room in her blue dress that fell into points like a hyacinth-bell and fluted out.

'Now, Margery . . . Margery Mannering. What are you doing *now*?'

They looked hard at each other; all the rest waited. Margery thought, 'She'd like to kill me.' Miss James thought, 'I would like to kill her – just once.' Her face had a hard wistfulness. 'Just *think*,' she gently invited. The girls in front turned round. Margery looked at her feet. Just feet, they were, like other people's; boat-like in dancing-sandals. Oh, she had taken the *third* position!

'Yes,' said Miss James and nodded. 'Now do you see? . . . Now you can take those positions again by yourself. – Music, please – Go!' The chords clanged vindictively, like choppers falling. '*Now* do you see?'

Margery had pretty-child affectations that sat for-lornly upon her. Now she flung back her hard curls; they bounced on her back. She peered up through misted spectacles like a plump small animal in the bite of a trap – like a rat, perhaps, that no one decently pities.

'Yes, Miss James.'

'Then please remember,' said Miss James, and walked away. The unrealized self in her made itself felt, disturbing her calm with a little shudder of pleasure. A delicate pink touched her cheekbones, she thought of Lulu, she was almost a woman.

Next the springing exercises, so graceful, from which the few little boys were excluded. Rows and rows of little girls kicking the air pointedly, showing the frills on their underclothes, waving their bent arms and fluttering fingers apart and together, tossing their heads. There were gleaning movements, throwing and catching movements, movements that should have scattered roses about the room. Miss Peel played 'Oh where, and oh where, has my little dog gone!' with a kind of saturnine prance.

Grizelda and Lois and Cynthia, Jean Jones and Doris excelled at varying movements; they were set to dance by themselves, to show the others. When someone was dancing alone as a glory the music was different, Margery Mannering thought; the choppers became curling feathers, fluttering in towards one and waving out.

The skipping began and finished; they passed the exercises with ribbons and Indian clubs. The fancy dances began. Little Cynthia was Spain itself in the Spanish dance; the grown-ups sighed at her, she was so sweet. Miss James told her that *next* Wednesday she could come, if she liked, with some castanets. Grizelda and Doris were best in the Irish Jig; so saucy, quite Irishly saucy. The Gavotte made two more couples illustrious; they were given the floor to themselves. 'If one could only teach you to curtsey,' Miss James sighed. If she could only, only teach them to curtsey. They went down on themselves all skewered; feet got lost behind them; knees stuck out in front.

'Just *look*, children: watch me' . . . But they all stood round sceptical; they knew they would never be able to curtsey like that. She sank with bowed head; with arms curved before her she melted into the floor. She flowed down into it and, flowing up again, stood. 'If I had a dress like that . . .' Doris thought. 'She's not like a person at all,' thought Jean Jones.

The hotel secretary stood looking in through the glass door. His eyes came a little nearer together, his face was intent. Miss Peel played a slow ripple; in her mind Miss James was curtseying.

After the fancy dancing there was an interval. The little girls flocked and slid to the chairs round the wall. Margery Mannering went back and sat by her grandmother's maid, who was knitting a bedsock. 'Got into trouble again, I see,' said the grandmother's maid and wetted her thin lips. 'You did ought to have practised that Spanish dance.' 'You mind your own business,' said Margery, who was rude to servants. She slid along three empty chairs and sat by herself. She watched Miss James go round the room, congratulating the mothers of little girls who had been dancing nicely. Governesses she did not congratulate; she was too tired.

Cynthia sat with her mother just beyond Margery Mannering; they were holding each other's hands excitedly and talking about castanets. Cynthia never seemed bare of being loved, it was round her at school, everywhere, like a sheath. Miss James came round to them, smiling. Margery watched, her head well back on her thick neck, playing with one of her ringlets, and Miss James felt something catch at her, going by. She had again that shudder of life in her; a quick light came into her eyes. 'Don't kick that chair,' she said, put on her smile again and went on.

Miss Peel was back at the radiator. 'How d'you feel?' she said. 'Must you go round all those hags? Are you bad?'

'I suppose I'll get through . . . Did you hear me killing that Mannering child?'

'Which one?'

'Oh, you *know*. The red one.' She laughed a little and sat stroking one of her arms. 'She makes me feel awful . . . I – I don't know how it is.'

'Has she got anyone with her?'

'Only a maid.'

'Perhaps she'll die,' said Miss Peel brightly, and ran her eye over a fox-trot.

'Oh, she couldn't,' said Miss James, startled. She couldn't do without Margery Mannering; she wanted to kill her. She got up and said: 'Now all take your partners for the waltz.'

'Lulu's been back,' said Miss Peel hurriedly. 'When are you going to see him?' Miss James shrugged her shoulders and walked off. The music began.

By this time the fog had been stained to solid darkness; the windows were slabs of night. The chandeliers were in full flower. Children went round and round, smoothly spinning; the tall looking-glass at the end of the room doubled them into a crowd; they were doubled again on the outside darkness. She could not think why nobody came to draw the curtains. When she felt him again at the door, looking in at her with that straight level look of desire, she went towards him, pulled open the door, and said, 'Do please draw the curtains. The room looks so ugly; the mothers don't like it. People can see in.'

'You will give up your train, just once, just tonight?' he said. 'Yes?'

'No, I can't, I'm tired; I've got a headache. Besides, you know Peelie's here; she wouldn't go home alone.'

He skirted the floor and went round to the three windows, touching a cord somewhere so that the curtains trembling with movement slid over them noiselessly. Returning, he brushed Miss Peel's back as she played. 'I want her tonight,' he said over her shoulder. 'We all three have supper together – Yes? I put you both into the 8.40. Yes? Dear Peelie, yes?'

She nodded, in time with the music.

'Dear Peelie – *good*!'

She wriggled her shoulders, he hurried away.

'All arranged,' he said joyously. 'I get a taxi immediately. We all three have supper together down by the Pier.'

'Go away,' Joyce James whispered. 'You're dreadful; you'll ruin me – *One* two three, *one* two three. *Time*, Jean and Betty, time, time! What are you doing! – Mollie, don't talk while you're dancing! Margery Bates, remember you're gentleman; what does a gentleman do with his hands? . . . *Toes*, Margery Mannering: *why* don't you *dance* on your *toes*?'

Lulu saw something wrong at the end of the room; the chairs were pushed crooked; he went to arrange them. Again he brushed past her. 'Till then, I keep watching. You are so beautiful. I would give my soul, my body, all that I have. . . .'

She walked away, clapping her hands together – '*One* two three, *one* two three,' watching the couples go round. Then she suddenly cried to the music, to all the children: 'STOP!'

Of course it was Margery Mannering. She did not know how to waltz; she went bumping and hopping round on the flat of her feet, with her partner all limp Miss James went over in silence and took her partner away.

'I shall have to take you myself. – All you others sit down for a moment. – We shall go on till I've taught you. And will you please *try*, Margery. You see you are wasting everyone else's time – Music, please!'

All alone on the empty floor, Miss James waltzed with Margery Mannering. They did not speak; they heard one another's breathing; the girl's light, the child's loud and painful. The thump of Margery's heart was like the swelling and bursting of great black bubbles inside her: now the bubbles were in her throat. Her hot body sagged on Miss James's cold bare arm. Her eyes, stretched with physical fear like a rabbit's, stared through the clouding spectacles at the mild white hollow of Miss James's throat. From her spectacles, light flashed up sharply into her partner's face as they circled under the chande- liers. Miss James's hand like a cold shell gripped the hot hand tighter.

'She really is patient and good,' said the mothers, nodding. 'She's so thorough.' They congratulated them- selves. 'Look at the pains she takes with that poor little stupid. Wonderful; she keeps smiling.'

And indeed, she was smiling. Lulu watched through the door; his eyes got larger and darker and closer together, his face came closer up to the glass. Miss Peel played on mechanically; she watched him watching.

'I'm giddy,' said Margery suddenly.

'It's no good. I shall keep you on till you've learnt.'

In the taxi, the girls leant back silently. Lulu, his back to the driver, sat watching the town lights flash over their faces. The fog was lifting, but the taxi went slowly through spectral streets like a blind snorting animal. Sometimes the driver pulled up with a jar; the girls nodded forward, the window-frames rattled. Joyce's close-fitting hat was pulled over her eyebrows; her half-hidden face was impassive. Peelie sat with her hat on her knees, she looked over Lulu's head, sombrely humming. Joyce rolled her head with a sigh and an impatient movement; Peelie and Lulu both reached for the window-strap; Lulu was first there and let down the window. Mist came curling in, the air freshened; the taxi had turned down through the old town and the lonely crying of sirens came from the harbour. 'They're awful,' Joyce shuddered.

'She *is* tired,' said Peelie to Lulu across her.

'She will be better after supper.'

'She won't eat,' said Peelie, discouraging.

'Won't you eat dinner?' said Lulu, imploring. He touched Joyce's knee, left a hand there. Peelie eyed the hand sharply. Joyce took no notice. Peelie's foot felt a gentle pressure. 'That's *my* foot.' 'Oh, so sorry, Peelie.' The taxi crawled past a terrace of balconied houses and sharply drew up.

The 'Star' Private Hotel was modest and friendly. It was six o'clock; they went in and sat in the lounge. Peelie was pleased at Lulu's discretion; *here* they would meet no one who'd recognize Lulu and Joyce and go away talking to make scandal about the Metropole dancing class. It did not do for Lulu, who showed ladies into their bedrooms, or Joyce who spent hours in clumsy men's arms, to be patently man and woman; their public must deprecate any attraction. Poor Lulu was also distressingly beautiful; the shabby other visitors kept turning round to look – at the grace of his height, his dark-ivory forehead (foreign men do so much more with a forehead), the ripple-back of his hair, his gaze of shy ardency Joyceward, narrowed by low straight lids. He went off to order the supper – just supper, they said, fish or something, with coffee to follow. Peelie shook Joyce's arm suddenly.

'Do wake up,' she said. 'Can't you really love anyone?'

'I didn't want to – you brought me . . . Well then, give me my powder-puff.'

'You've got heaps on – it's colour you want. Haven't you got——'

'No, you know I don't have any; Majowski hates it.'

'You may be thankful Lulu's Swiss. He wouldn't let you just sit there yawning if he were an Italian.'

'No. He's going to keep an hotel – isn't it awful. With two private funiculars. On the top of a glacier or something. Oh well, *he* won't melt any glaciers!' Joyce changed a yawn to a laugh; she laughed weakly, ruefully, almost in spite of herself, biting in her mouth at one corner and shrugging her slight shoulders.

'What are you laughing for?' said Lulu, coming back. They did not answer; he showed them into the dining-room. The room was empty, not a waitress there. He guided them to their table with an arm lightly round Joyce's waist; as he pulled her chair out she had to step back closer against him. Peelie's hard unabashed eyes contemplated them curiously. Each conscious of the two others they waited, then something in Peelie's eyes made it impossible, shameful for him not to press Joyce closer and kiss her twice on the cheek, high up, where the patch of colour sometimes appeared. Peelie laughed, Joyce laughed uncertainly, Lulu uneasily smiled: they sat down. Joyce unfastened her coat and let it slide down her shoulders, showing her neck and the soft rucked top of the hyacinth dress. Her eyes glittered under the hanging lights with their cold white shades.

'Did you see me killing that child?' she asked Lulu, eagerly turning. 'You were there at the door, you must have seen. Wasn't I dreadful – Peelie thinks I was dreadful.'

'Which child?' he said, while his eyes asked doubtfully, 'Who's there? What's there? *Are* you, at all? I want you.'

'Tell him, Peelie.'

'That fat Mannering child with red hair, she means. I only said: "Don't hate her so's the others can notice." '

'But I do hate her, don't I? Isn't it awful of me. I made her waltz till she cried. But I did teach her.'

Peelie eyed her exaltedness. 'She's quite awake now,' she said, congratulatory, to Lulu. 'I daresay she's quite hungry.' But soon the film crept back, Joyce faded like the roofs into this afternoon's mist; she let her hand lie coldly in Lulu's under the table. As Jean Jones had thought, she was not like a person at all.

When supper was finished they strolled back towards the harbour to look for a taxi. The salt air was milder, lamps made pale stains on the mist. It was high tide; under the mist, to their left, the dark, polished water sucked hard-lipped at the embankment. The edge of the road was protected by chains slung from posts; Peelie went to look over, stood idly clanking and swinging the chain with her knee.

'I wonder what you two would do next if I fell in and never bobbed up again.'

'Oh, *Peelie*!'

'Well, I won't – not *this* woman. All the same, I do wonder. . . .'

Her meditation, tinged with contempt for them, broke up sharply when, hearing no more behind her, she turned to see where they were. Lulu had caught Joyce out of the lamplight . . . He was not so unlike an Italian. They stood as one figure till with a gasp he stepped back from her. Joyce stood vaguely, huddling up her coat-collar and looking round for Peelie. They started towards each other under the lamp. Peelie thought: 'Now what's coming?' but all Joyce said was: 'We must get that taxi. I can't go any further. Oh, Peelie, I'm *dead*!'

It was a long drive from the harbour up to the Central Station. No one spoke. Lulu's hands hung between his parted knees; he kept wringing and chafing his hands together. Joyce slipped deeper, deeper into her great fur collar, a swerve of the taxi flung her on Peelie's shoulder; she did not stir, she leaned there inert, asleep. Peelie slipped an arm along the back of the seat; supporting her; this was how they were going to travel home. Light from a picture-palace blared in, disturbing them like a trumpet-blast, on to the small set face of the sleeper, her hat pushed down unevenly over one eye. Lulu, startled, cried out: 'It's not fair!'

'Hush! . . . Nothing's fair.'

'In six weeks I go back to Switzerland. What does she care? – Nothing. And still you are having her day after day.'

'You and I, you and she, she and I, we'll forget each other anyhow – that's nature.'

75

'Don't you care?'

'Not so much.'

'Peelie. . . .'

'Um?'

'*Peelie* . . . I . . . let me just. . . .'

She beckoned. Two or three minutes were taken up
by a cautious shuffling, balancing, edging; they rose
and changed places like people passing each other in a
boat. She sustained Joyce's weight till his arm touched
her own, supplanting it, under Joyce's shoulders. Joyce
never stirred, never woke; she lay quiet under their
movements, their whispers and anxious breathing.

'Don't touch her head, you'll wake her – *don't*, Lulu;
just let it roll – I do – it finds its own place. Just keep
your arm – so – loosely; keep your hand on her other
side so's she won't flop back . . . You'll be as stiff as hell
in a few minutes – I am, always. Don't try moving,
that's worse; just relax. . . .'

Joyce sighed; her sleeping body crept closer against
him, her head rolled into the hollow of his shoulder –
'found it's own place'. She sighed again with her cheek
on his breast; she was comfortable here. Lulu's face
came down, scarcely breathing; his chin was just over her
little black hat.

Joyce smiled. A new life, the self's, moulded her
lips in a soft line. Her face was all broken up, vivid in
sleep . . . She was dancing with Margery Mannering.
'I'll kill you, I'll kill you,' she said like a knife. Something burst behind Margery's stretched eyes; she
fainted . . . Joyce smiled in her sleep.

AUNT TATTY

T H E train stopped every ten minutes after it left the junction: each time Pellew jumped up to clutch his hat and stick in a spasm of nervousness. The screech of brakes, the jolt that passed down the coaches repeated themselves in his vitals. Each time the white station palings, the lamp and the porter slid into view again he would gulp, put a hand to his tie and experience once more that sense of fatality. At the back of the station for Eleanor's home there was a group of beeches; their beautiful bare green trunks like limbs stood boldly out in the February sunshine. He stepped from the train and stood staring: they were so beautiful they were a kind of escape, yet they brought round again his yearly chagrin, his suspicion of being cheated. Then he remembered Eleanor – if he could be said to have forgotten her – and turning, saw her a few feet away, blinking, a thin colour creeping up her face.

'Hullo – Paul.'

'Eleanor . . . splendid!'

'Splendid!' They shook hands. He couldn't remember when they had last shaken hands; he supposed when they had been introduced. He looked down, sideways, at the little fiery crocuses spurting against the fence.

'I've never seen crocuses in a station before,' he said hurriedly. 'Wallflowers, of course, and stocks. I . . . some railways offer prizes. . . .'

'I saw you looking at the beech trees, too,' said Eleanor, with a triumphant, informed little air, as though she had stolen a march on him. They walked down the platform together towards the barrier. They each told themselves that they must avoid any show of emotion with people, Eleanor's neighbours, about – but *wasn't* Spring . . . As Paul tasted the air and coming out on to the road saw the pale fields washed over with sunshine, with knolls of trees rising here and there like islands, he tingled. He hated constraint – this business, this effort ahead. He wished he could have come down and spent the day here alone. Eleanor wore – as a kind of symbol – a straw hat, new-looking, pulled down over her eyes, but her shoes were wintry, heavily covered in mud; she had splashed mud over her ankles up to the edge of her skirt. In spite of being so thin she looked womanly and capable, a regular country girl, and he couldn't believe he had held her crushed in his arms, helpless. London altered her, he could only suppose.

She walked fast, swinging along with a stick. She was embarrassed and silent. More tentatively than by an inspiration he wheedled her into a copse by the side of the road, put his stick down and threw his arms round her. A blackbird fluted, all round little crumpled primrose-leaves were pushing up through the beech mould. She strained her face away, showing the fine line of her jaw; he felt her go rigid against him under her bulky tweed coat. 'Not here,' she cried, 'not here, don't; it's like the village people. Don't, Paul!'

It was in the country, Paul knew, that his shortcomings began to appear. He wasn't a gentleman. He wore a grey suit, but it did not look right somehow. His technique was all wrong; he should not go further than Chiswick or Richmond – unless to the Continent. He reached for his stick philosophically. 'As a matter of fact, my dear,' he said, startled to frankness, 'there seemed nothing to say.'

She emerged from the copse ahead of him, cautiously, and went on rapidly down the road.

Down the avenue Eleanor's mother came strolling to meet them. Paul braced himself. His position was perfectly simple, he was Mr. Pellew, a friend of the Jennings' (Eleanor's friends in town). He had met Eleanor with them. He just happened to be in this part of the world, seeing churches. He had suggested himself to luncheon and they had sent him a friendly reply.

'Seeing churches' – Eleanor's mother beamed on his cultivation. Diffuse yet stately, she had Eleanor's fine hardness with an alloy, melted over the edge of the mould, running into a form of its own, a privileged kind of formlessness. Little girls – they resolved themselves into three – came running out of the bushes and slung themselves on to Eleanor's arms. Young sisters.

They brought with them out of the bushes some kind of a gummy smell; twigs and little pieces of young leaf clung to their reefer coats and their pigtails. 'Scaramouches!' said their mother, contented. They stared at Paul politely but indifferently, as though he did not come into their world at all. Paul thought: he would show them. He wondered whether it would be big-boyish and popular – brotherly – if he were to tweak their pig-tails but he dared not; these were not town little girls; one never quite knew.

Eleanor seemed pervaded all at once with an anxious vexation. She kept glancing sideways – across him – at her mother's profile. She pulled little bunches of grey buds off the flowering currant trees and crumbled them between her fingers.

'You live in London,' said Eleanor's mother positively.

'I suppose in a kind of way I do.'

'So much going on there,' sighed Eleanor's mother with a polite affectation of chagrin. 'One's terribly out of it . . . Patsey, run on and look for Aunt Tatty. I can't think where she's gone to' – A child sped away – 'Mr. Pellew will be hungry. Do you write about churches?'

'Mr. Pellew doesn't write at all,' said Eleanor sharply.

'So many people nowadays do.' The mother wrinkled her brows up; she had got him all wrong, he wasn't an author at all; now there would be all this fearful business of readjustment. She turned to Paul with a gesture and laughed despairingly, confidentially, lovably. He laughed back, the remaining little girls tittered. Still laughing, they passed round the bend of the avenue into sight of the house.

The sun struck full on the square façade and in at the windows, which with their blinds half down had an appearance of blinking. Tufts of winter jasmine grew at the foot of the steps that went steeply and massively up to the open hall-door. Two puppies asleep at the top twitched, yawned, stretched and came bounding down curved like bows. They made straight for Paul and jumped up; they remained on their hind legs, propping their rigid fore-paws against his knees, grinning ineffably. 'Nice fellows then, nice boys,' said Paul, brushing them off politely.

'Don't they give you a welcome – dogs do *know*,' said Eleanor's mother.

'I should be sorry to think they did,' said Paul genially.

He looked sideways at Eleanor, who stiffened. She said with just old stimulating perversity, that inflection . . ·
'As a matter of fact, Mr. Pellew doesn't care for animals.'
'Fancy!' said Eleanor's mother.

She wandered about the drawing-room, from table to table, showing him bowl after bowl of spiky leaves. He wandered after her. 'Hyacinths?'
'Oh no; I hate the waxy smell. They're unhealthy, I always think. These are tulips – muscari – daffs. They'll be out in a week. I had early tulips by Christmas.'
'Had you really? Eleanor, you are terribly un-exotic.'
Eleanor had taken her hat off; she showed her crisp, light-brown hair brushed sidways across her forehead, her thin face with the jaw a shade prominent, the nose so adorably crooked, her dark, rather deep-set eyes; her whole expression eager, serious, immature. Her smile, which came doubtfully, was also a little crooked; this crookedness lent it the air of a greater complexity than her nature possessed, of ruefulness, of subtle uncertainty, of the constant re-weighing of values. She was slender and strong-looking; she stooped.
She smiled when he said she was un-exotic. 'Nobody said I was.'
'That's what so——'
' – Oh, please hush! I don't think the door's shut.'
He shut it; the feeling of being shut in together evidently frightened her. 'Do remember,' she said, 'you're just someone who's come to lunch. Do be natural – like anyone of that sort would be. And don't – don't *look* at me, Paul. You make me so ashamed and uncomfortable.'
'Ashamed?'

'Oh, it's not that mother would notice, but it seems all wrong here. You see this is my home, Paul, and it's me too, what I've always been . . . Do open the door again. It's so . . . well, you know. Shutting ourselves in. I'm only supposed to be showing you the bulbs and the Bartolozzi.'

'Ah yes,' he said, 'and I haven't seen the Bartolozzi, have I?' He made no attempt to open the door again, so she opened it herself, doggedly.

'Then I can't really see,' he said in a low voice, 'why I've come down at all. You won't hear of my having it out with them all; you won't let me touch you——'

She winced. 'You don't understand,' she said. 'It was different in London. But here – I do hate feeling . . . common.'

'I'm sorry,' he said, 'I'm a man, you're a woman. Love is rather common, I dare say.'

'Don't be so intellectual!' she said bitterly. 'Do be more human – and give us all time. Can't you do what you promised? Make friends with them all. Be something more than just a man. Make mother feel you're real. Be jolly with the children, like the other men who come here.' ('Evidently,' thought Paul, 'I *ought* to have tweaked their pig-tails.') 'Then tell mother yourself about us – when she's had time to see for herself.'

'Everything?'

'Of course not – it would sound terrible put into words. I think mother would die. Just say you began to like me when I was in London.' She stood with her face turned away from him, listening distractedly all the time for a possible step in the hall, speaking confusedly.

'So you're ashamed, on the whole, of what happened in London?'

82

'It seems so unreal. It's got no background. It isn't what one could possibly build up one's life on.'

They heard steps at last, coming downstairs and beginning to cross the flagstones. Eleanor brought out a bundle of knitting from behind a cushion and sat down, swinging her legs, on the end of the sofa, with her shoulders clad in a fluffy blue jumper hunched forward a little. She frowned at her work like a schoolgirl, chaste and negative. Paul wheeled round to study the Bartolozzi engravings which, more than a dozen, hung in a pattern all over one wall. Chintz-covered chairs were drawn up to the fireplace in a semi-circle; the women of the family would sit thus, looking up at the mantelpiece where the men, the brothers killed in the war, the dead father, the brother in India, stood lined up in their silver frames, staring out at nothing frankly and fearlessly. The family jaw repeated itself. The pendulum of the Dresden clock swung lazily, the fire rustled, Eleanor's needles clicked.

' "One's life",' he impatiently thought. 'This is living, O Daughter of the House, this is how time passes, this is how you approach death!'

A lady with white hair piled up on her forehead came in, preceded by one dog and followed by another. She glanced at Pellew a moment, penetratingly over her rimless glasses. 'Eleanor,' she said in a deep voice, 'you haven't introduced this Mr. Pellew to your Aunt Tatty.'

Eleanor hated, evidently, this failure in social alertness. Aggrieved, she performed the introduction. 'Mr. Pellew,' she added, 'is a friend of the Jennings'.'

'I know, I know,' said Aunt Tatty; 'you told me that twice. I'm not such an old lady.' She ran her eyes over him candidly, so intelligently that he shifted his attitude.

He felt for the first time that morning in touch with a fellow-being, at once on guard and at ease. 'I hear,' said she, 'that all you friends of the Jennings', their what they call "set", are remarkably clever and modern. Splendid for Eleanor – I should be quite out of touch. Do you care for the country?'

Paul looked out of the window for reference. 'Depends,' he said guardedly.

'I daresay,' said Aunt Tatty, and glanced at his knees. 'Too bad, the dogs have been jumping up. You should control your dogs, Eleanor, they are impossible. We shall never have modern visitors . . . Dogs,' she added, in explanatory aside, 'are a habit, I think.'

Lunch went through with strands of talk spun out fine till they dwindled to thin little patches of silence. Pellew, his back to the fire, sat between two young sisters and Eleanor watched him. 'Have you got a pony?' 'Oh no, we ride horses . . .' 'Isn't that pretty!' (pointing to a coloured prism falling from the water-jug). 'What, that? Haven't you seen one before?' 'The colours . . .' 'I don't care for violet,' said the younger sister, wrinkling up her nose. 'Do you keep rabbits?' 'We did, but they died. Do you?' 'I used, but they died too.' 'Oh! I didn't know men kept rabbits.' 'That was when I was a little boy.' 'Oh.' They were here to eat not to talk and they turned from him politely and finally. 'All their lives,' thought Paul, 'they'll go on eating slabs and slabs and slabs of roast mutton. . . .'

Eleanor's mother came in to lunch with a pile of literature which she placed on the table beside her. She kept fingering leaflets. She was longing to talk to

Aunt Tatty about the Women's Institute. Every now and then she would draw a long breath and lean over vaguely towards her sister-in-law. He could see thought struggling up from the depths of her mild eyes. Then she would recollect him. She kept 'bringing him in'. 'It is a great movement,' she told him, 'a great movement. Here, we have taken up basket-work. We are so keen. But I don't suppose,' she faltered, her eyebrows knitted again in despair at herself, 'that you'd know very much about basket-work! One gets so absorbed – terrible. It isn't like architecture. Do talk to me about churches. It would be lovely to know. . . .'

Aunt Tatty listened impartially. She sat with her shoulders a little shrugged, the weight of her body tilted; when she was not eating it seemed that, below the edge of the table, her hands were clasped on her knees and she were leaning upon them. She looked round at her relations as though she had not yet wholly identified herself with them, still had the faculty of seeing them. Yet she had an air of being permanently among them; she didn't exert herself. Whenever Paul looked at her she always seemed to be looking at Eleanor. She was a stoutish, aristocratic old lady in a 'good' black. During a longer pause than usual, while the mother fingered her leaflets and Eleanor stared at her plate, she said to Pellew:

'Do tell us about the Jennings.'

Ursula Jennings (Maltby before her marriage) had been a school friend of Eleanor's. He thought of her as a dark young woman, at her ease everywhere, emphasizing without declaring herself, reserved, daring, patronizing, subtle, discreet. Indescribable. He didn't, as a matter of fact, care for Ursula Jennings. He had 'owed her one' for her manner ever since that first evening, with Eleanor. He didn't believe she cared for Eleanor really. He had always known William and couldn't at the moment, from sheer nervousness, visualize him. Fattish . . . sceptical? Good on Venetians – seventeeth century? That wouldn't say anything *here*. He put himself into the Jennings' drawing-room, determined to build them both up from the outside, detail by detail, but all he saw was Eleanor getting up from a gold chair under the red lacquer lamp, uncertainly, with her curiously square, pale face; thin, awkward, serious, eager, to hold out her hand to him. He felt startled, a little angry as though someone had touched him, and said in an abrupt voice:

'I haven't seen anything of them lately.'

Eleanor's mother put down a brochure on rabbit-keeping. 'But surely . . .' she objected, 'Eleanor said you'd been there so much.'

'I mean, not since then.'

'That was only three weeks ago,' said Eleanor's mother, gently informative, smiling.

'In London, I expect,' said Aunt Tatty, 'people who are all friends, who are "a set", see each other almost every day.' She twinkled her spectacles at Pellew and smiled knowingly.

Pellew, standing in the open door at the top of the steps, waved an arm at some trees and exclaimed, 'Those are – splendid!' They did not, it is true, burn in like the station trees – he was tired now and could not receive impressions so sharply. These were not bare beech, stretching up full in sunshine, but elms with the sun behind them. A slight wind, imperceptible in the shelter of the house, tossed their branches so that the sky behind them twinkled. It was towards the end of the afternoon; the wheels went round more easily but he drooped, he could feel them all drooping, with social fatigue. They had paraded the garden and the paddocks; feeling high-pitched, he kept pulling them up to indicate and exclaim at what nobody else saw.

'Yes, that's our barn roof – that's moss makes it so green. Yes, isn't it green. What were you going to say?'

'Nothing. Only it's *so* green. With that light on it.'

'Yes, it is green . . .' After a little glance across at each other, a slight pause, they would pass on.

Embarrassment kept prevailing. Pellew felt an awful bounder. He wasn't used to being entertained, he kept initiating, he couldn't go properly passive. He tried to make his mind slack as an empty sack to be trailed along, but he couldn't; there was something in it that kept catching on things, bumping. He walked between Eleanor and her mother (Aunt Tatty had stayed in the house to write letters). They hesitated along the garden borders, stopping, lifting here and there a leaf with the point of a walking-stick and bending down to peer under it. Meanwhile he stood behind them and yawned, stretching his whole being. He looked along the espaliers, up at the brick walls, down at the turned soil and blunt-tipped enamelled noses of young plants poking up through it, and yawned again. 'Life,' he thought, 'life!' Gravely Eleanor picked him a crocus which he gravely put in his button-hole. She walked bare-headed with her bare hands deep in her coat-pockets; keeping close beside her he slipped his fingers into a pocket and touched her wrist. Feeling the muscles contract in a shiver he thought with surprise: 'So she loves me!'

Now they were back on the steps again; her mother

had gone in murmuring something, sighing. 'Those trees . . .' he repeated, pensively, with a kind of inspiration to the inept.

Eleanor said at last, 'I suppose we *feel* the country; we don't——'

'Aestheticize about it?'

'You do rather, don't you.' Absently and kindly, like a sister, she put a hand on his shoulder and leant a little upon it. 'I do care for you,' she said, frowning at the elm trees. 'It's so difficult, isn't it? Don't be discouraged.'

'I thought *you* were. I should have liked so much to have kissed you – just once.'

'Do I seem awfully different?' she asked wistfully.

He looked back over his shoulder into the hall. All round the doors stood ajar letting in panels of afternoon light; in the drawing-room window, Aunt Tatty was at a writing-table, silhoueted against a strip of sunny lawn. Loyal to Eleanor's privacy, it was for him to say rapidly, 'Hush!' She drew into herself, the hand slipped from his shoulder, there flitted across her face an expression of disappointment. He had rebuffed her.

'If you'd care,' she said with an effort, 'I'll show you the church. You may as well see *one* church, I suppose,' she added, smiling unhappily. 'Do you know, Paul, till your letter came I hadn't had to tell a lie for three years. I remember the last quite distinctly; it was something to do with Aunt Tatty's coffee, when we were abroad. I hate lying – I wish I were not such a coward . . . Would you dare, do you think, after all, speak to mother tonight?'

She was taking him to the church by a way of her own; down an overgrown track through a thicket. He went ahead, parting the interlaced branches of hazel and willow and holding them back for her. They walked unsteadily over tussocks of pale, wintry grass and desiccated bracken. 'I'm afraid,' he objected, 'we've made that rather difficult, now. Are you so certain, then, that they like me?'

She didn't answer, only stared at him.

'You see,' he said gently, 'I'm not at all their sort. I'm not your sort, really. I'm afraid you'll have to get used to the idea of their not liking it.'

'It's hard at present, naturally. We're not in the way of new people.'

'I'm too new. There's nothing to go on. I'm all in a void. I'm a phenomenon for them.'

'Paul——'

He strode on a few feet ahead of her, speaking over his shoulder, pressing his way through the branches. She cried his name again, and as he gave no sign of hearing came hurrying after him. 'I do care, I do!' she exclaimed with a catch in her voice; 'I feel in a thicket everyway. Yet I have been happy; I came back from town feeling dazed. I prayed you might write, though I'd made you swear you wouldn't. Paul, I'm yours, honestly – look at me.'

He stepped back and put his arms round her, not ardently as he had done in the morning but with a queer mixture of diffidence and desperation. He caught one passionate and frightened look from her eyes before she closed them. 'Now we're alone,' he said, 'listen to me, Eleanor. How do you feel . . . Wouldn't you come back to town with me now, come abroad, and we'd write to them from there? Married – I meant married. It's nothing desperate we both want to do, after all; I wouldn't be spoiling your life – a life's what I want to give you. I've made myself some sort of a place in the world, I've a good deal of money. They'd get used to me afterwards. Wouldn't you come?'

'Why like that, why——'

'It's the only chance. Oh, I'm not so uncivilized really. I'd wait any time, please anyone, if I were sure of you at the end. But I couldn't be, all this is sapping us. At the end of some more of these days there wouldn't be anything of us left. We have been real people – we *are* real people, at the back of us – somewhere. And you're great; it's that that I've felt in you. Don't make life an affair of behaviour – you try but it isn't.'

'What is it then?'

'I don't know – why make it anything? – let it make you something. Will you come back with me?'

'Why must I come?' she cried miserably. 'It's not fair to make me decide. I don't know what's real; all today I've been absolutely bewildered. It's so difficult. I can't even imagine mother – afterwards. It might kill her, or she might hardly be worried a bit——'

' – All tomorrow,' he said, 'they'll be pulling me to pieces gently. They won't even know they're doing it, but there will be nothing left of me – and nothing in you could survive it. They couldn't tell you a thing about me I haven't told you myself, but to hear them say it would absolutely finish me for you. We wouldn't see each other again. You must decide. I felt today: this is going to be the crisis, I felt it as soon as I saw you there on the platform, more when we met your mother, most of all when we came into the house. "Think what your brothers would have thought" – that would be your mother's last shot. I shouldn't have got on well with your brothers, Eleanor.'

'I do like you for saying that – but I think you're wrong.'
She added in a matter-of-fact voice, as though the ideas
had followed each other in natural sequence: 'I'm
coming with you – only look, Paul, what shall I do? – I
haven't a hat.'

He was so much startled, he laughed aloud. She
smiled, and they stood staring at one another, trans-
formed by this one wild moment. The afternoon light
came slanting on to them through the branches, they
were trellised over with thin definite shadows which
moved to and fro, to and fro as the branches tossed. The
thicket closing round them with its damp, mossy smell,
its tunnels of blue shadow, might have been a forest
through which they were roving unhampered. He cried
'Beautiful!' and they kissed spontaneously and eagerly,
as though meeting again. With her hands on his
shoulders she looked about her triumphantly, at her
lover, at the trees, as though she were having her own
way at last, as though this idea had been hers and only
the opposition had come from him. 'I can't go back to
the house,' she said; 'I must buy a hat on the way. I'll
wait here and you walk down to the village, to the Green
Man, and hire a car. There are new people there who
won't know me. Then we can drive to the junction.
We can't go up by the slow train, feeling like this, and
it wouldn't do to wait about at our station. Don't let's
lose time, Paul. Come quickly.'

'Where does this path lead? Where are we going?'

It was a short cut that bisected the avenue some yards
ahead. She slipped an arm through his own and was
hurrying him along; she no longer smiled; she looked
very serious and exalted. Her profile, the hair blown
back from her forehead, made him feel he was running

away with a Joan of Arc. They stumbled over the tussocks; in his hurry he stepped on the first primrose he'd seen that year, deep down in its leaves in the middle of the path. He did not realize how close they were to the avenue till Eleanor, without caution, had hurried him half way across it. Then he glanced to his left, stopped dead and said softly, 'Done in.'

Aunt Tatty, strolling from the direction of the house, had hailed them and was cheerfully waving.

'Having a look round the place?' called Aunt Tatty.

Eleanor, also turning, took her hand from Paul's arm and vaguely stared at her approaching aunt. She seemed less confused than utterly taken aback. Aunt Tatty advanced without embarrassment; possibly she had seen nothing. She wore an astrakhan coat and a decided-looking felt hat; grey Shetland muffled the amplitude of her chin.

'Don't you feel cold, Eleanor, wandering about without a hat? Seems to me it's turned chilly. I'm just taking your mother's letters and mine to post, for the sake of the walk – Will you come with me?' she turned to Pellew. 'I could show you the post-office. Pretty, but not much in the way of architecture – Eleanor, your mother's been looking for you.'

While Paul watched, something in Eleanor faded. As though at the suggestion from Aunt Tatty she shivered faintly and turned up her coat-collar. 'Don't go!' he said sharply and clumsily. 'You promised,' he insisted, holding her eyes, 'to show me the church.'

She looked blank. 'I think, Mr. Pellew,' interposed Aunt Tatty, 'that while Eleanor's mother is looking for her we mustn't detain Eleanor.'

'In half an hour I'll be at the church,' said Eleanor,

and, without looking again at her aunt or her lover, walked away in the direction from which Aunt Tatty had come.

Pellew wondered if just such blind black moments as this preceded murder. He found himself moving forward numbly, sucked in the wake of the stout lady. She was in full sail again, with the invulnerable complacency of a man-of-war. Yet at the very crisis of his sickness and anger there was something grateful in this contact after the aloofness and erratic fires of Eleanor.

'Fancy not having looked at the church yet,' Aunt Tatty was observing; 'wasn't that what you came for? But of course,' she went on, 'one could see that it wasn't that. You two are in love with each other, aren't you?'

Pellew began laughing awkwardly, with self-derision. 'Were we so unnatural?'

'I could guess beforehand – Eleanor is quite transparent. It occurred at once to her mother, even, although she, as I dare say you noticed, is a good deal vaguer than I am. Churches,' sniffed Aunt Tatty – 'of all the childish inventions – *Churches!*'

'I'm an architect by profession, you know,' said Pellew stiffly.

'Oh, I dare say you may be,' said Aunt Tatty, and looked at him keenly. 'But that doesn't explain, you know, why you couldn't be more direct with us. Why you couldn't have declared yourself frankly, or have let Eleanor confide in her mother – You *do*, I suppose, mean to marry her?' she sharply added.

'Of course,' said Pellew, surprised by her manner, by her queer alternations of irony and bustle. 'But I do, of course, anticipate trouble. Well, as you noticed at once, I'm not Eleanor's sort. Not any of your sort. I feel up against so much in her here that I never suspected. If I'd guessed what it was going to be like here, I wouldn't only have *funked* coming down, I wouldn't have come at all——'

'Wisest not, perhaps——' said Aunt Tatty.

'All my feeling is for her as a woman. Socially, I find her difficult. Socially, she seems to find me impossible.'

'Really – is that really so, now?' Aunt Tatty said eagerly. Suddenly flushed, she seemed annoyed all at once by the warmth of her muffler, which she loosened with quick little tugs, poking out her pink chin impatiently over the folds.

'Not an easy basis for marriage,' she said dogmatically, with a queer note of triumph. '*I* didn't marry on that,' she informed him, '*I* wouldn't. And I might have at one time, there were a good many reasons . . . besides some affection on both sides. But I didn't. Later on, I married much better. Of course I had plenty of opportunities. Which is more,' said the Aunt complacently, 'than Eleanor may have.'

'That does make a difference.'

His irony was lost upon her preoccupation. 'I have sometimes wondered——' she began, then suddenly broke off.

'Really?'

'I was rather wild at one time,' admitted Aunt Tatty. 'Intellectually, I mean,' she qualified hastily, touching the brim of her hard hat. 'I hesitated; I suppose I was quite unhappy. He was nothing socially; quite young, but there was promise – brilliancy. But the promise,' cried Aunt Tatty triumphantly, 'didn't fulfil itself. I'd been right all along. He went downhill in every way – rapidly.'

'Disappointed, perhaps?'

'Faugh!' said Aunt Tatty. 'One disappointment! . . .
So you see I've had nothing to regret. There's no pro-
tection in life like a lack of courage. I've been a happy
woman, Mr. Pellew.'

Something unreal in her tone, some lack of simplicity,
made him say with a touch of impertinence, 'You are
to be congratulated.' They were approaching the lodge
gates. 'Come out into the open,' she said, sardonic and
genial, 'take your chances.'

'Which, quite frankly,' he said, 'you think are the
worst in the world?'

'In so far as Eleanor is my niece, they'll be as bad as
I know how to make them. In so far as you're a clever
modern young man whom I quite like – well, I couldn't
wish you anything better than to be clear of the lot of us.
In so far,' she concluded, wistfully genuine, 'as my own
curiosity is concerned (for I tell you, I *have* sometimes
wondered –) I shall be sorry to see the end of this so
soon. I should like to see what became of you both –
though I'm perfectly certain, of course, how it must end,
your marriage.'

'So you'll fight me over it?'

'Certainly.'

'By conviction?'

'By conviction,' she assented, loudly and definitely;
a sharp sigh heaved up the lapels of astrakhan coat.

'Fairly?'

Silently, she handed him her letters. He took them
and pushing through the lodge gates crossed the road
and slipped them into the postbox. He stood a moment
more with his back to her, mustering his forces, before
he dared to turn round. She had remained leaning back

on her walking-stick, watching his every movement, taking him in, measuring him with intensity. 'Fairly?' he asked again, coming back, raising his voice to be heard above a sudden clamour of rooks. He stared straight with some kind of a pang, a sharp conflict of confidence and antagonism, into her hard vivid face. She had touched the man in him.

'Yes,' said Aunt Tatty with a little laugh and braced herself, 'Fairly.'

'Then come back to the house,' he said. 'There is something I must say, at once, to Eleanor's mother.'

DEAD MABELLE

T H E sudden and horrible end of Mabelle Pacey
gave her a publicity with the European press
worth millions to J. and Z. Gohigh of Gohigh
Films Inc., Cal., U.S.A. Her personality flashed like a
fused wire. Three-year-old films of Mabelle – with
scimitar-curves of hair waxed forward against the cheeks,
in the quaint creations of 1924 – were recalled by the
lesser London and greater provincial cinemas. *The
Merry Magdalene* – Mabelle with no hair to speak of,
in a dinner jacket – was retained for weeks by 'The
Acropolis' and 'The Albany' wide-porticoed palaces of
the West End; managers of the next order negotiated
for it recklessly and thousands had to be turned away
during its briefer appearances in Edinburgh, Dublin and
Manchester. The release of her last, *Purblind*, was
awaited breathlessly. Her last, when brimming with
delighted horror, horrified delight, with a sense of fore-
knowledge as though time were being unwound from
the reel backwards, one would see all Mabelle's unconsciousness under the descending claw of horror. Nothing
she had ever mimicked could approach the end that
had overtaken her. It was to be, this film, a feast for
the epicure in sensation; one would watch the lips smile,
the gestures ripple out from brain to finger-tips. It was
on her return from the studio at the end of the making
of this very picture that she had perished so appallingly.

The management of the Bijou Picturedrome at Pamsleigh considered themselves fortunate in having secured *The White Rider*, a 1923 production. Since dusk, on a framework erected above the façade of the picture-drome, green electricity scrawled 'Mabelle' in the rainy sky. She was with them for three nights only; the habitués streamed in; uncertain patrons, pausing under her superscription, thumbed the edge of a florin, looked up and down the street, and when the metal ticket finally clicked out, dived still two-thirds reluctant into the stifling tunnel of tobacco fumes and plush. From half-past five, for half an hour before the first showing, the entrance curtain never settled down into stillness; at half-past eight another rush began.

William Stickford's afternoon at the Bank went by distractedly. He was intelligent, solitary, self-educated, self-suspicious; he had read, without system, enough to trouble him endlessly; text-books picked up at random, popular translations, fortnightly publications (scientific and so on) complete in so many parts, potted history and philosophy – philosophy all the time. On walks alone or lying awake in the dark he would speculate as to the nature of reality. 'What am I – but *am* I? If I am, what else is? If I'm not, is anything else? *Is* anything . . .' He would start awake, sweating, from a nightmare of something that felt like an empty barrel rolling over the ups and downs in his brain and bumping into craters that were the craters of the moon, or of going round to the house where he lived to pay a surprise call on himself and being sent away with a head-shake, told point-blank he had never been heard of here. Sometimes – an idle but anguishing sport of the mind – he told himself he was the victim of some practical joke on the scale of the universe of which everybody and everything, from the stars and the Manager to the pipe-cleaners, tooth-soap and bootlaces fringing his existence, were linked in furtive enjoyment.

He never 'went with a girl'; his landlady deplored this; to do so, she said, would make him more natural-like. She liked a young fellow to *be* a young fellow, and William apparently wasn't. His Manager, a kind unperceptive old man who believed in the personal touch, asked him up for a musical evening to meet his nieces, but William achieved being shy and aggressive, looked askance round the side of his glasses, snubbed the nieces and couldn't relax with the Manager. The girls discouraged their uncle from asking him home again. A fellow at the Bank called Jim Bartlett succeeded in knowing him up to a point; *he* couldn't get Jim quite into focus but he supposed he liked him all right. Jim would force his way in of an evening, paw his books with a snigger of admiration and sit with his feet on the fender and the soles of his boots steaming till twelve o'clock, till one's brain went stiff and dry. Theoretically, William needn't have listened, but he did listen; other existences tugged at him with their awful never-dismissable, never-disposable of possibility, probability even. Sometimes Jim forced him out. William was cinema-shy, he resisted the cinema till a man with important-looking initials mentioned it in a weekly review as an 'art-form'; then he went there with Jim and saw Mabelle. 'I can't think,' Jim had said, that first evening, impatiently gathering up his change at the box-office, 'how a lot of this girl's stuff ever gets past the censor.' William expected Mabelle's appeal to be erotic and went in armoured with intellectuality, but it was not erotic – that *he* could see.

The film had begun; with a startled feeling he had walked down the tilted gangway towards Mabelle's face and the dark-and-light glittering leaves behind. A caption: 'Can't you believe me?' then a close-up: Mabelle's face jumped forward at him, he stepped back on to Jim's toe and stared at a moon-shaped white light in an eye, expecting to see himself reflected. He stood for a moment, feeling embraced in her vision. 'Confound you!' said Jim and pushed him sharp to the left. They waded through to their places; William sat down, shaken, and put up a hand to his eyes. 'It's beastly jumpy,' he said, 'I always heard they were jumpy.'

'You get used to them – Gosh, what a lovely girl, isn't she? – Look at that, old man, look at that for a figure!'

It had been all very abstract, he recognized in it some hinterland of his brain. He understood that passion and purity, courage, deception and lust were being depicted and sat there without curiosity, watching Mabelle. That was some five months ago, before her death; she had long been known to the connoisseur, but her real vogue was only then beginning. She had an unusual way with her, qualities overlapped strangely; in that black-and-white world of abstractions she alone moved in a blur. Each movement, in unexpected relation to movements preceding it, outraged a preconception. William sat with an angry, disordered feeling as though she were a rising flood and his mind bulrushes. She had a slow, almost diffident precision of movement; she got up, sat down, put out a hand, smiled, with a sparklingly mournful air of finality, as though she were committing herself, and every time William wanted to rise in his seat and say 'Don't, don't – not before all these people!' Her under lids were straight, she would lean back her head and look over them. Her upper lids arched to a point, she had three-cornered eyes; when her face went into repose the lids came down slowly, hiding her eyes for moments together. When she looked up again that dark, dancing, direct look came out as it were from hiding, taking one unawares. It was as though she leaned forward and touched one.

William, who suffered throughout from a feeling of being detained where he had no business, was glad when the film was over. He said on the way home, 'She's awfully different from what I expected, I must say.' Jim Bartlett responded Aha!' He kept saying 'Aha!' with an infinite archness and refusing to volunteer much about Mabelle himself. 'She's got temperament,' was the most William got out of him. 'You know what I *mean*; temperament. Jolly rare thing. She ought to play Iris Storm in *The Green Hat*.' That night it was William who wanted to bring Jim in and keep him talking. Not that Jim's ineptitudes were any more tolerable, but he had a feeling of someone at home in him, in possession, very assured in the darkness, mutely and sardonically waiting till he was alone.

A week or so later he saw in the local paper that *The Fall*, featuring Mabelle, was showing at Belton, ten miles off. Eluding Jim, he bicycled that same evening over to Belton. He pedalled furiously, mounting the steep sleek high-road over the ridge, his brain a cold clamour of self-curiosity. Enlightened shamefully, burning, he bicycled home in the teeth of an icy wind. Next morning, cornered by Jim's too pressing inquiries, he lied as to where he had been. It had been Jim's fault, he shouldn't have asked him.

Thought, as he understood thought, became pale and meaningless, reading scarcely more than a titillation of the eye-balls. Lapses appeared in his work. He was submerged by uneasiness, alternately, as it were, straining after a foot-fall and slamming a door.

There was this thing about Mabelle: the way she made love. She was tired, oh fearfully tired. Her forehead dropped down on the man's shoulder, her body went slack; there seemed no more hope for her than for a tree in a hurricane. When her head fell back in despair, while the man devoured her face horribly, one watched her forgotten arm hang down over his shoulder: the tips of the fingers twitched. What was she thinking about, what did women think about – *then?*

One night Jim Bartlett, routing about among William's possessions, pulled out *The Picturegoer* from between some books and the wall. On the cover Mabelle, full length, stood looking sideways, surprised and ironical, elegantly choked by a hunting-stock, hair ruffled up as though she had just pulled a hat off, hand holding bunched-up gauntlets propped on a hip. Jim, shocked into impassivity, stared at the photograph. His pipe sticking out at an angle from his expressionless face reminded William of a pipe stuck into a snowman.

'Pretty photograph, isn't it?' said William aggressively, to shatter the bulging silence.

Jim removed his pipe thoughtfully. 'Upon my word,' he began, 'upon my *word*! You really *are* you know. I mean really, old man——'

'I got it for you, as a matter of fact. If you hadn't gone messing about I'd have——'

'Oo-hoo,' said Jim, 'we don't think. No, *don't* think——'

'Then don't think. And damn you, get out!'

They were always very polite to each other at the Bank; there was little coarse talk or swearing. Jim Bartlett was very much shocked and went home. Next morning William apologized. 'Say nothing more about it, old man,' said Jim nicely. 'I quite understand. Beg yours, I'm sure. If I'd had any idea you were going to take it like that——' Good-feeling made him perfectly goggle-eyed. He came round punctually that same evening to hear all about it. William was out; he remained out till half-past eleven. He did this three evenings successively, avoiding Jim at the Bank, and after that Jim didn't come any more.

If William had been open and manly about the business, as pal to pal, Jim Bartlett would have been discretion itself. As it was, in the course of events, he told all the other fellows. They told the Manager's nieces, who told the Manager: the Manager soon had occasion to speak to William seriously about work and excessive cinema-going. This concentration of interest upon him, of derision, hardened him outwardly, heightened his sensibility. He avoided the 'Bijou' at Pamsleigh, the 'Electra' at Belton, but took excursion tickets to London and saw Mabelle there. Expeditions to the remoter suburbs were often necessary, he would sup or take tea dazedly in gas-lit pastry-cooks' and wander between showings of the film through anonymous vacant streets. Life all these months rushed by him while he stood still.

William never looked at his newspaper before lunch-time; others did. One morning, coming to the Bank he was aware of a tension, of a scared shy greediness in the others' faces, of being glanced at and glanced across. Jim Bartlett came up once or twice, looked strangely,

flinched off, cleared his throat and kept on beginning –
'I say . . .'

'What's up?' snapped out William, exasperated by
what seemed a new form of persecution.

'Nothing much – seen the paper?'

'No.'

Jim Bartlett, driven and urgent, fidgeted round in a
semi-circle under the blank and intense glare of William's
glasses. 'There's something – look, come home to dinner.'

'Oh, thanks, I don't think so,' said William in the
consequential sleek little voice he'd assumed. Jim
tugged at the lobe of a crimson ear helplessly, shrugged
a 'So be it, then', and went off.

In his sitting-room, the *Daily Mail* was propped
against William's water-jug. Mabelle's name blazed out
over the centre column, with 'Fearful Death'. With a
sudden stillness, with a feeling of awful, extended leisure,
William put out his hand for the paper. While he read
he kept putting his hand up and touching his throat.
Each time he did this he started as though he had
touched someone else, or someone else had touched him.
He read carefully down to the end of the column,
looked over the top of the paper and saw his chop slowly
congealing behind it. He ran from the room and was
violently sick. When this was over he took up the paper
again, but he couldn't read well, the lines bulged and
dipped. He waited a little to see if he was going to be
sick any more, then went out and bought all the other
papers. Coming out of the news-agent's he met the
wind tearing down the street. He stood on the kerb-
stone, not knowing which way to go; the wind got into
the papers and rattled and sang in them; they gave out
an inconceivable volume of sound to which he believed

the whole town must turn round and listen. He looked this way and that, then pressing the papers against him ran across the street and went into the church. Here he read all the other versions. Physical detail abounded. He sat for a long time crushed up to a wall in the gloom of a pew, then went back to the Bank.

Five weeks later, *The White Rider* featuring Mabelle Pacey came to Pamsleigh. 'Going?' said Jim to William, who seemed to have 'got over things' wonderfully well. 'Oh, I dunno,' said William, 'I've some work on at home' (he was doing one of those correspondence courses), 'I don't know that I've got time.'

On Monday and Tuesday he did not go to the Picture-drome; he disappeared utterly, no one knew where he had gone. The last day of Mabelle was Wednesday; Wednesday came.

The afternoon at the Bank went by, then, distractedly. Rain fell past the tall windows blurring the outlook, the trickle and stutter of drops racked the nerves. With dread, William looked up at the clock again and again, uneager as never before for release, half hoping by some resolution, some obduracy, to staunch the bleeding-away of the minutes. The door to the back passage was open for some minutes; William kept looking away from it, and while he was looking away Mabelle stood there, leaning a shoulder against the lintel, smiling and swinging a gauntlet. She was confident he would be there tonight. He faced round to the empty doorway. Mightn't she as well be *there* who wasn't anywhere? Who was not. She was incapable now of confidence, of a smile, of pressure against a lintel. He had faced for these last weeks her absolute dissolu-

tion. At that reiteration, in his mind and the doorway,
of emptiness, he must have made some movement or
sound, for the others looked up from their ledgers.
William coughed and showed himself as in some agony
of calculation; the faces dropped. The afternoon dwindled
out, the office shrank in the dusk and began to be crowded
with shadows. Somebody climbed on a chair with a
taper; the gas coughed alight and the rain sliding and
streaming down the window-panes scintillated against
the thickening night. Woven securely into the room's
industrious pattern William rested, but now the pattern
was torn up violently into shreds of clamour and movement. They all went home. William lingered over his
ledger a long time, but was finally drawn out after them.

At ten past eight he was pushing against the 'Bijou's'
interior curtain. Its voluminousness, a world of plush,
for some moments quenched and smothered him; a
prickly contact to hands and face, exhaling a warm dank-
ness. The attendant fought him out of it, taking away
his ticket. 'Standing room only!——' he grudged her
her little triumph, he had been told that outside. He
chose a place along the transverse gangway and gripped
with hands still pricking from the plush a cold brass rail
behind the expensive seats.

He looked down a long perspective, a flickering arcade
of shadow. For twenty seconds or so there was no one –
the trees' fretful movements, the dazzlingly white
breaking-through of the sky. The orchestra wound off
their tune with a flourish and sharply, more noticeably,
were silent down in their red-lighted pit. The flutter
and click of machinery streamed out across the theatre,
like the terrified wings of a bird imprisoned between two
window-panes – it gave him the same stretched sensation

of horror and helplessness. A foreign whiteness, a figure, more than a figure, appeared; a white-coated girl on a white horse drawn sideways across the distant end of the drive. She listened, all tense, to that same urgent flutter and clicking, then wheeled the horse round and dashed forward into the audience, shadows streaming over her. William recoiled from the horse's great hammer-head, the hoofs dangerous as bells, the flick of the eyeballs. He looked up with a wrench at his being; advancing enormously, grinning a little at the moment's intensity, Mabelle looked down. They encountered. Visibly thundering, horse and rider darkened the screen.

Gripping the bar tight, William leaned back to look up at the bright, broadening shaft from the engine-room directed forward above him. Along this, fluid with her personality, Mabelle (who was now nothing) streamed out from reel to screen, thence rebounded to his perception. It was all, her intense aliveness, some quivering motes which a hand put out with intention would be able to intercept. The picture changed focus, receded; Mabelle, in better perspective, slipped from her horse and stood panting and listening; the horse turned its head, listened too. Their sympathy, their physical fineness, sent a quiver across the audience. In protest, a burst of assertion, the music began again. '*Tum* – tirumti *tum* – turum ti *too*, rum ti *too*——' Mabelle tied her horse to a tree and turned off cautiously into the forest.

The man was there, in a glade, that man she generally acted with, whom one had a dozen times watched her make herself over to, her recurring lover. He stood with his back to a tree, with a grin as of certainty, waiting for her. However much he might repel at the outset, however craven, false or overtly lustful he might show himself, he had her ultimately, he had to have her, every film. She liked her men fallible (evidently); unsympathetic to audiences, subject to untimely spasms of passion. It brought out all her coolness, her lovely desperation, her debonair fatedness. Her producer kept this well in mind. With unavailing wariness she now came stepping with her white-breeched legs, the light glancing off her riding-boots, high over the fallen trees, low under the overhanging branches. Shadow struck off her head again and again. The man smiled, threw his cigarette away, stepped round his tree and closed with her . . . A poignant leap-back, one was shown the white horse standing, tormented by intuition, tossing its head uneasily, twitching its ears.

William had come late, the end was sooner than he expected. Mabelle in a black straight dress, in meekness and solitude, stood by a high stone mantel looking into a fire. The preceding caption was red, the light now tinged with a realistic redness. Flames, in leisurely anticipation of their triumph, spurted and leapt at her feet; the firelight fingered its way up her, crept round her arms' fine moulding, her throat, her chin, with curbed greed, assurance, affection almost. She stood there – to the eyes of that four-years later audience – dedicated. It was as though the fire knew . . . A log crashed in, she started, looked with appalled eyes away from the fire. She was waiting.

Oh, *Mabelle* . . . She was too real, standing there, while more and more of her came travelling down the air. She seemed perpetual, untouchable. You couldn't break that stillness by the fire; it could shatter time. You might destroy the film, destroy the screen, destroy her body; this endured. She was beyond the compass of one's mind; one's being seemed a fragment and a shadow. Perished, dissolved in an agony too fearful to contemplate (yet he had contemplated it, sucked meaning out till fact had nothing more to give), she returned to this, to this imperishable quietness. Oh, *Mabelle*. . . .

Somewhere a door opening, light that lanced the darkness. Movement went through her like the swerve of a flame. She held her arms out, the illusion shattered, she was subject once again to destiny. William sharply turned with tight-shut eyes. He groped his way along the guiding bar, was at fault a moment, collided with the attendant looping back the curtain for the exodus. He went out slowly, into the glaring vestibule, down the three steps into the lit-up, falling rain. Rain brushed his face, drops here and there came through to the roots of his hair. He put his hat on; heard the drops, defeated, pattering on the brim.

The street, unreal as that projected scene, was wide; he hesitated half way across it, then slowly turned to the left. Behind, inside the open doors, he heard as it were a wave break, a crash of freed movement, a rasping sigh. The band played the National Anthem. Feasted with her they all came streaming out, and she, released from their attention, dismissed, dispelled now – where was she?

His way home was at an angle from the High Street, up a by-path. Water in the steep gutters hissed and gurgled. There were spaces of inky darkness, here and there some lamplight dimly caught a patch of humid wall. He looked back, once, towards the town and the Picturedrome. One moment 'Mabelle' was blazing emerald over the white façade; the next the lights were out, 'Mabelle', the doors beneath, had disappeared. So she went. In another month or so, when her horror faded and her vogue had died, her films would be recalled – boiled down, they said. He had heard old films were used for patent leather; that which was Mabelle would be a shoe, a bag, a belt round some woman's middle. These sloughed off, what of her? 'You're here,' he said, and put out a hand in the darkness. '*You* know *I* know you're here, you proud thing! Standing and looking. Do you see me? . . . You're more here than I. . . .'

Going blindly, he passed within inches of a pair of lovers, plastered together speechlessly under the wall. A too urgent pressure had betrayed them by the creak of a mackintosh. Love! His exaltation shuddered at the thought of such a contact. Then for a moment under the blight of that dismal embrace, he had lost her. Mabelle . . . *Mabelle?* Ah, here. . . .

Here, by him, burning into him with her actuality all the time. Burdening him with her realness. He paused again where a bicycle with lighted lamp had been leant up against some palings. The murky dark-yellow light streamed across the rain; some ghostly chrysanthemums drained of their pinks and yellows raised up their heads in a clump in it, petals dishevelled and sodden. As he watched, one stem with its burden detached itself and swayed forward, dipped through the lamplight and vanished. He listened and heard the stem snap. How – why – while the other stems stood up erect and unmoving, sustaining their burden? *Who* had——?

Oh no, not that! He began to be terrified. 'Don't press me too hard, I can't stand it. I love you too much. Mabelle, look here – don't!' He looked beyond the chrysanthemums, left and right, everywhere. She was there, left, right, everywhere, printed on darkness.

William, at home in his sitting-room, walked about in a state of suspension, looking, without connection of thought, at his books and pictures. A clock struck twelve, it was already tomorrow. *This* morning he'd be at the Bank, back again in the everyday, no one the wiser. Now he could sleep a short time, then life, that abstraction behind the business of living, was due to begin again. *He* was alive, enclosed in a body, in the needs of the body; tethered to functions. In the gaslight it looked rather shabby, this business of living. Greasy stains on the tablecloth where he'd slopped his dinner over the edge of his plate, greasy rim round the inside of his hat where he'd sweated. This was how one impressed oneself on the material. And on the immaterial? – Nothing. Comfortless, perilous, more perishable than the brains in his skull even, showed his structure of thought. He had no power of being.

Of feeling? Only that life was worth nothing because of Mabelle who was dead. And by death, had he hope that he wouldn't quench himself utterly while Mabelle, who impinged herself everywhere, brightly burned on?

The right-hand top drawer of his bureau was empty of what such a drawer should contain: the means to the only fit gesture that he could have offered her. He had jerked the drawer open with an unconscious parade of decision, an imitation, more piteously faithful than he was aware, of something which, witnessed again and again under the spell of that constant effusion from Mabelle, had seemed conclusively splendid. The hand slipped, unfaltering into the back of the drawer, the gesture of pistol to temple, the trail of smoke fugitive over an empty screen. . . .

He was denied this exit. Under the stare, vaguely mocking, of three-cornered eyes he bent down to study the note-books, the bitten pencil-stump, match-ends, attempt at a sonnet, a tie, crumpled up and forgotten, that littered the drawer.

THE WORKING PARTY

COMBE FARM commanded the valley; it had a road of its own, gated across to keep the cattle from straying, that ran down past the mill and parallel with the river till it came to a full stop at the barn doors. The house was three-storied, old and solid, with an irregular line of roofs; it stood out remarkably with its group of poplars over the flat fields of the shallow and empty valley. A line of willows followed the meandering of the river.

Mrs. Fisk, up at her bedroom window, could see down the road for a long way. When by twos and threes, at first very indistinctly and slowly, the Working Party came into sight her heart leapt to her mouth and she could hardly contain herself for apprehension and pleasure.

The road looked white and staring under the bright March sky; the women in their brown, black and navy afternoon dresses walked in the middle sedately. The thin unending dark line of them dotted itself away down the valley. Presently their voices began to be heard; one could see that they were carrying work-baskets. Now they began to be as conscious of Combe Farm as Mrs. Fisk was of them; their eyes no longer wandered, they stopped talking and each put on a remote expression as though she were walking at large in a desert. Mrs. Whales, Mrs. Tuppett and Mrs. Miller headed the procession; at the dim end one could recognize Miss Vincent, wobbling along on a bicycle between the cart-ruts.

The Working Party had met throughout the winter at the homes of members, turn by turn. The Lodge, the Vicarage, over the International Stores . . . Tea was provided. So far, it had not come to Combe Farm because that poor little thing Mrs. Fisk had been really too recently married. Also (ostensibly) because the walk down the valley was too long for short afternoons. So she had eaten tea in all manner of parlours and had taken particular note of the way it was served. She had noted the china, the teaspoons, the doylies and saved herself up to outdo them. Then she invited the Members to meet at Combe Farm.

When at last she heard the latch of the gate click Mrs. Fisk, who was twenty-one, went down on one knee for a moment by the large mahogany bedstead and prayed that all might go off well – nay, showily. Her husband was out with the men in some distant fields, the farm-yard and house were quite quiet; she and the Working Party were to be absolutely alone. She listened a moment over the banisters, preening out the frills of her blouse, then went downstairs jauntily.

Since before dinner she had been in a turmoil: ever so busy. For two days she had kept the parlour fire burning to expel that uneasy chilliness wont to settle upon the room. The parlour faced south-east, the sun went off it early, which made it beautifully cool in summer but in the afternoons at other times of the year a little sad. It was a room in which she never felt comfortable but always entirely ladylike. She picked double daffodils that had come out under the south wall and

settled them along the mantelpiece in the ruby Bohemian
goblets given her by her grandmother. The daffodils
lolling forward looked at her frowsily; she did not feel
pleased with them and wondered why she had been such
a silly girl and not gone for sprigs of flowering currant
instead. It would be just like her to do something stupid
and ruin the Working Party. In an earlier fit of self-
distrust she had decided against making the cakes herself,
she had gone into town on the bus and bought dainty-
looking sugary ones with crystallized flowers – *gâteaux*.
She had been to a new shop where she paid sixpence
each more for them than anywhere else where they
called them cakes. She turned the cat off the fur rug,
then coaxed it back because she remembered that someone once said cats looked cosy. The cat came nimbling back
on the tips of its paws and looked at her scornfully. She
climbed on a step-ladder to loop back the curtains at the
top and let in more light, then she felt dizzy up there and
screamed. Her husband, who happened to be passing
across the kitchen, had to come in and help her down
again. He kissed her – they had been married so
recently – but she struggled from his arms in a pre-
occupied way, like a cat, and hurried away to blow dust
off a fern.

He was a busy man and a farmer, his mind always
wrinkled up tight and knotted with other concerns.
He went away from her without even a sigh, he never
so much as wondered . . . By midday, when she should
have been feeding the chickens, she was still walking
about the parlour, biting the tip of her tongue. She
couldn't make up her mind what to do with the tablecloth. She knew perfectly well that the Working Party
needed a bare table to cut out on and scatter their

pins over, but she couldn't bear to take off her chenille
tablecloth. It was the loveliest green with a bobbly
fringe, with a pile on it like an Axminster carpet and
a sheen like corn; when one stroked it against the light
its colour deepened. She decided to leave it there till
they were all gathered round and had had a good look
at it, then whisk it off with an exclamation as though she
had forgotten it. She moved a photograph of her own
wedding group further forward so that they should all
see her standing there with her 'sheaf' in her beautiful
lace dress. She couldn't feel now, however, that her
wedding-day *had* been so very important.

Phyllis the maid was down in the kitchen cutting
platefuls and platefuls of bread-and-butter and sandwiches.
She had never managed to cut them so thin before;
she came up very much flushed to open the door for the
Working Party, blowing back wisps of hair from her face
and brushing the crumbs from her hands. She was stout
and pink and her apron was most gratifyingly clean –
Mrs. Fisk stood watching her critically through the
crack of the parlour door. Abruptly, with a swing of both
arms, Phyllis headed the Working Party into the parlour.

All in a dream Mrs. Fisk shook hands with them couple
by couple and invited them to sit down. She still had a
feeling that several of them must have got into the
room somehow and be walking about *without* having
been shaken hands with. None of them would remain
sitting, more and more came in and the room became
crowded and dark like a wood from the numbers of
women standing up in it. The cat got up and walked
away from under their feet; it would not stay still and
look cosy. Mrs. Fisk poked the fire, then all at once the
room seemed too hot and she felt a sudden and violent

need to open a window. The Vicar's wife sat down at last and this seemed a signal; in a moment or two only Mrs. Fisk was left standing, her clasped hands pressed to her chin in anxiety, very conspicuous over the sea of hats like Combe Farm over the valley. They settled down with a creak and a slippery sound on the leather chairs, opened their work-baskets and stared at each other doubtfully.

'We can't get very far with the tablecloth on, Mrs. Fisk,' Mrs. Tuppett said warningly. She drew her long upper lip down and blinked over the top of her steel-rimmed glasses as though she had known from the first there was bound to be a hitch somewhere.

'Tck – tck – tck – ,' Mrs. Skinner said patiently, looking round the room to see how different it was now and taking particular notice of the Bohemian goblets.

Mrs. Fisk stood with her hands to her chin, all in a daze struggling to come out with her exclamation.

'There now!' she whispered at last with an effort. She couldn't get near the table because of the women sitting round it so closely. 'Such a *pretty* cloth,' said Miss Vincent, and, running her finger along it, admired the sheen. She said with a sigh, 'It's as soft as pussy-willows.' The clumps of pussy-willows along the valley were golden at present, yet Mrs. Fisk felt somehow insulted. Miss Vincent and the Vicar's wife folded the tablecloth corner to corner and hung it over the back of a chair. 'There now!' said Mrs. Fisk, again, watching them. Under the cloth the table, polished this morning, had been awaiting its moment; now it reflected the hands and faces moving above it, the square of the window, the wicker sides of the work-baskets. The basket-lids lolled from their hinges, turning up their tight plump satin-upholstered bosoms, scarlet and olive-green, bristling with pins and needles and splitting across in lines from very exuberance. The work was unfolded, scissors clattered about on the table, and now and then a reel of cotton escaped from its mistress and bowled away happily. Now that the Working Party was actually working, Mrs. Fisk could not believe her eyes.

Mrs. Fisk, alert as a fawn in a thicket, took up her work and began to herring-bone. Her stitches were large and eccentric, but she did not feel responsible for them. Every time she looked at her work she seemed to be missing something, yet whenever she paused with her needle up in the air and looked round her she seemed to be the only one idle. They were all very satisfied-looking and serious. She was the youngest there except for Euphemia Wolley. Euphemia sat by the fire sewing with a short thread and looking down her nose at her needle; her eyelids never so much as trembled whatever anyone said and her pale-blue felt hat was pushed to the back of her head at the most superior, I-don't-care-about-*you* kind of angle. Her needle, slanting one way with precision, zip – zip – zipped along the hem of a bed-jacket. Mrs. Fisk and she had taught at the same Sunday school, and now for very spite she wouldn't so much as look round the parlour or take the least notice of anything. A flush spread slowly over her face from the tip of her nose and she seemed to despise everything that had not to do with bed-jackets. Mrs. Hawke from the Lodge had the whitest neck in the world with a seed-pearl necklace nestling into a crease of it. She was so sympathetic and friendly that her face looked quite anxious and was never entirely vacant of one of its little smiles: before the last faded someone else would have said something and, though it might not be addressed to herself, Mrs. Hawke never let anything pass without her own little pat at it, an understanding and tender smile. She was so nice to oneself that one was outraged at seeing her being equally nice to everyone else. She seemed to have perfect confidence in her fair waved hair which crimped out in little curtains under the sides of her hat, for she never once put up a hand to it. Mrs. Fisk was determined to ask her to stay behind when the others had gone, to look round the garden – perhaps, one never knew, they might have a real talk. She only wished there were anything in the garden to offer Mrs. Hawke or, for the matter of that, anything special for her to look at.

Mrs. Whales was speaking; the lapels of her afternoon blouse were drawn together across her full bosom with a cameo brooch. 'I didn't think I'd be able to come today,' she told them. 'I'd been that put about over Marion. The spring brings her out in a rash all over and it makes her fretful. But I didn't like to miss a meeting, even though it *was* difficult. I haven't missed one meeting, you see.'

'Neither haven't Mrs. Tuppett nor I,' said Mrs. Miller.

'You *have* been splendid,' interposed Mrs. Hawke, 'I only wish I had been more regular.'

'Ah well,' said the Vicar's wife indulgently.

'Well, one likes to do what one can, what I mean,' said Mrs. Miller, and shook out a bed-jacket.

'I must say,' said Miss Vincent, 'I shall be *sorry* when the meetings are over. Though I must confess,' she added mysteriously, 'that this afternoon, I very nearly turned back. Can you guess why?'

'Ah! Cows?'

Miss Vincent nodded. 'I don't seem able to get over it. Awkward, isn't it? Of course a bicycle helps; I always feel I could run round to the other side. But I've been like that ever since I was quite a tiny. I must confess, I've never been up the valley before. One would be so much alone if anything were to happen.'

'Our cows wouldn't look at you,' said Mrs. Fisk scornfully. She had no use at all for Miss Vincent. 'I like them myself, they're company.' She thought, 'How like an old maid!'

Miss Vincent said eagerly, 'Oh, I dare say it is a bit lonesome for you. It's very pretty down here, but it does seem a long way from everywhere.' The others assented; they glanced nervously at the window as though they expected the solitude outside to come walking in.

Mrs. Skinner gathered up her work on her knees and sat with her mouth open a moment in reminiscent silence. 'Poor Mrs. Fisk that *was*,' she brought out, 'Mrs. Fisk senior, couldn't keep a girl here anyhow. She often complained to me: "It's the place", she used to say. I was most intimate with your poor mother-in-law, you know, Mrs. Fisk. She said to me shortly before she died, "I can't keep a girl anyhow". Of course she did the greater part of the work herself, but she needed help with the fowls. Oh, she was very much troubled latterly, poor soul. Nothing seemed to go right with her. I often said, "I do pity you, with all my heart I do". She was such a good soul – it seemed quite a happy release.'

'*I've* had no difficulties,' said Mrs. Fisk and tossed her chin. The idea! She was wearing an emerald, crêpe-de-chine blouse with frills and a gold wrist-watch and must look, she knew, quite a different kind of a Mrs. Fisk to

William's poor mother who had petered out while *she* was still at school. Everybody looked twice at this Mrs. Fisk, who was tipped with pink like a daisy on cheeks, nose and chin. A Working Party at Combe Farm in those days would have been a very different affair. 'No difficulties,' Mrs. Fisk repeated firmly, and Euphemia Wolley bit off her thread with a twang.

The Vicar's wife standing up to cut out some more sleeves paused a moment to gaze at Mrs. Fisk. She had yearning watery eyes, no children, and a flat, disappointed-looking figure. She had taken off her coat and stood leaning forward, in her plain shirt draped across with a watch-chain, one hand on the small of her back where the pain was, the other pulling her scissors open and shut, open and shut, like a hungry beak. She was spiritual-looking and might have been the patron saint of all the Euphemias. 'Very lucky, my dear,' said the Vicar's wife, and her tone said: 'That is not the lot of the human soul . . . that is not the lot of woman.' Then she cut out three pairs of sleeves and some pockets while the others drew in their work-baskets to give her more room on the table. Mrs. Fisk, a shade chilled, felt once more like a confirmation candidate and wriggled her feet together. The clock ticked the first hour away, then broached the second. Now and then a clamour of starlings arose in the garden; later the cat caused a diversion by reappearing suddenly and getting on to Mrs. Hawke's lap.

Tea was timed for four-thirty. Mrs. Fisk, face to face with the clock, watched the hands jealously lest time should escape her. She once more divided the number of people into the number of cakes. She pictured the tea-tray as it ought to appear, in the doorway, being carried in. She did wonder if Phyllis would remember the silver strainer. She had never used a strainer – she and Phyllis enjoyed telling each other's fortunes from the tea leaves round the insides of their cups. She did wonder whether, after all, paper lace doylies might not look daintier under the *gâteaux* than crochet ones.

She wondered – Unable to bear separation from Phyllis at this crisis she got up with a murmur, squeezed round carefully past the back of the workers' chairs and crept from the room. She listened a moment, outside, to the imperturbable, strenuous buzzing; then, with a tremendous feeling of ownership, closed the door on her bees.

The kitchen was sunk a little into the foundations of the house at the back, half its depth below the front rooms. Eight steps went twisting down to it, at an angle, from the back of the hall. When the kitchen door at the foot was shut the steps were pitchy, it was like running down into a well. A half-moon of ground glass, very high up, strained a little light through, but this faded away in a patch on the opposite wall. Half way down Mrs. Fisk, going precipitately, clutched at a banister and pulled up short so that she swung forward a little. There was (as she felt in that half moment that she should have expected) Somebody there.

A man sat on the steps below her, crumpled against the banisters. His back curled forward in a horrible way, one shoulder dropping to meet a knee that was clumsily doubled up. While she watched (perhaps because of the tug she had given the banisters) he fell together; a booted foot slid forward over the edge of a step and went clattering down the two next. The other shoulder, wedged in tightly between the banister-rails, kept the rest of his body from toppling after the foot.

'Dead,' thought Mrs. Fisk, with the same sense of disgust and irritation with which she would stoop in the rainy dusk to pick up the sodden corpse of a chicken. Gathering in her skirts she crept downstairs past him, shoulder against the wall. At the bottom she pushed open the kitchen door to let in more light and looked up with peremptory anger, as though she expected the thing to account for itself. 'Dead!' she said angrily. 'There now!' It was Cottesby the cow-herd, and she saw the whole thing very lucidly. Cottesby the cow-herd, a greyish-faced man, had 'a heart'. For years he had threatened this; the idea of his end had seemed to be a companion to him. He had never liked her; he looked at her from under his cold shadow sanctimoniously and coldly. She noticed that in a last spasm he had ground his face into the banisters. His neck was twisted, his nose poked slyly out between two of the rails and the same two rails indented his forehead. 'At any moment,' thought Mrs. Fisk, 'he'll come tumbing on top of me.' She stepped back into the kitchen.

Phyllis sat with her apron over her head, her fists blindly drumming on the edge of the kitchen table. There was little that Mrs. Fisk did not know about hysterics; she directed herself with cold violence against the quivering bulk beneath the apron. The attack had, she realized, its justification. Phyllis had found herself cut off from the approach to the parlour by the appalling presence of Cottesby. It must have been Cottesby's intention, feeling death upon him, to seek out the Working Party for succour. He had come in by the back door and crossed the kitchen; at the foot of the stairs he had been overtaken. Mrs. Fisk gave thanks to Heaven for so merciful an intervention. She snatched a water-jug, she slapped at the clawing, pink hands and heaving shoulders. Phyllis let out staccato noises like a steam-engine; she was being a thousand times more troublesome than Cottesby and it seemed a pity she had not died also. 'Shut up, you great gawky!' her mistress cried. 'Do remember the ladies!' She splashed another handful of water in Phyllis's face. 'Stay quiet, will you!' she thundered.

'I will, m'm,' said Phyllis, and hiccoughed. She was better already.

The kettle-lid leapt suddenly, a jet of white steam spouted across the kitchen. Mrs. Fisk, still red with anger, recollected herself mechanically. Her silver urn and teapot stood with their lids back, open-mouthed. 'What of it?' asked Mrs. Fisk, cold with defiance, and made the tea. Phyllis had finished cutting the bread and butter; the trays were ready; the *gâteaux*, violet, pink and orange, sat consciously upon their crochet mats. They looked very well. Mrs. Fisk stared hard at them; she felt them communicate their composure. Nothing should wreck her.

She went to the foot of the stairs again and looked up. There was no doubt about Cottesby. His nose stuck out further than ever and a half-shut eye looked past it out of the shadows. '*You* won't run away,' said Mrs. Fisk grimly, and indeed he could very well wait. Death, physically familiar enough to her, appeared at this moment supremely improper. She thought of Euphemia Wolley and set her teeth. Nothing should wreck her. She was a lucky one . . . She had told them all she was a lucky one. '*I've* had no difficulties,' she had said, and tossed her chin.

She measured out the distance between the wall and

Cottesby. He had left her room to walk up past him, carrying the trays.

As the clock's hands crept down to half-past four the Working Party began to relax. The needles dawdled; many were unthreaded frankly and stuck into bosoms or work-basket lids. Garments were passed to and fro for admiration and comment; conversation languished. A dazed look came into the workers' faces, as though the afternoon were a dream; they shifted on their chairs and one or two yawned.

'Time flies, doesn't it,' said Mrs. Skinner in an aggrieved voice because she wished it were more than twenty-past four. Mrs. Fisk's absence seemed to her natural and encouraging; she was sitting close to the door, she listened, they all listened. Mrs. Hawke, still sewing, looked up and smiled sympathetically though nobody had spoken. 'Well I must say,' confessed Mrs. Whales, surprised at herself, 'I for one shall be glad of my tea.'

They heard the tea-tray, the light elegant tinkle of silver on china, cup slipping on saucer, that is like no other sound in the world. Mrs. Fisk came in, arms wide, chin high over the urn. She was flushed, it was a great moment; even Euphemia looked at her. She was out of breath, her green jabot shifted as her chest went up and down, but she was perfectly calm. She explained that her Phyllis had been called away on a message. She did not seem to think that it mattered. Everybody had seen her Phyllis, everybody knew she *had* a Phyllis, nobody minded. They helped her replace the green tablecloth.

Her teacloth had a lovely gloss on it and a six-inch border of pillow lace; she shook it out of its folds with a gesture and laid it on diamond-wise. She was very much at ease with them all – one might say, patronizing. She shook back her frilly cuff to glance at her wrist-watch: half-past four to the minute. She shut the door carefully after her when she went out for the second tray – funny, when that gave her all the trouble of pushing it open again! When she came back she was red and white in sudden patches, as though her face had been painted.

'I declare,' she said ('Laughing' they remembered afterwards 'ever so'), 'I nearly tripped up on the stairs. I'm so unaccustomed to carrying trays . . . Milk *and* cream, Mrs. Hawke? . . . Mrs. Rudd, sugar?'

Once a lump slipped from the poised sugar-tongs into the milk-jug, splashing her blouse. It was her sole misadventure. She sat at the head of the table, under her own wedding-group. She thought privately that *gâteaux* were the sandiest things she had ever eaten: nothing but sponge inside with a thin acid layer of cream. However, they were diminishing rapidly. Mrs. Hawke appreciated the yellow plum jam and might be persuaded to take a pot back with her. Wondering whether Phyllis would break out again (she had locked the back door and brought the key up with her so's Phyllis couldn't escape *that* way) – wondering whether she and William would be suspected, arrested, she kept offering everybody more tea. Her tea-tray looked lovely, Mrs. Hawke's own couldn't beat it. Nobody else had such an artistic tea-service with garlands of mauve wistaria. At a moment when everybody was talking she thought she heard sounds in the back of the house. This might be Cottesby, coming unstuck from the banisters, rolling down into a heap by the kitchen door.

She clattered the lid of the urn. Euphemia Wolley, biting a slice of mauve *gâteau*, was staring across at her. How Euphemia would turn up her eyes if they came in and took one away. 'I hope that violet *gâteau* is to your taste, Euphemia?'

The vicar's wife didn't eat cake in Lent; she had finished her tea and she sat listening for something far off with the saddest expression. 'I *do* so well remember dear Mrs. Fisk senior,' she said in an interval. 'I had tea with her here when I very first came, as a bride. She had made everything on the table herself, I remember; the bread, the butter . . . I did think her wonderful. Afterwards she took me into her kitchen and showed me her beautiful copper pans. Have you still got those beautiful copper pans?'

'Oh indeed yes,' said Mrs. Fisk, 'Mr. Fisk has had several offers for them, they are very much sought after. But Mr. Fisk won't hear of parting from them, for the sake of association.'

'Association!' tittered Mrs. Whales. 'Aren't they still used for preserving?'

'Very occasionally,' said Mrs. Fisk with reserve, and turned her eyes down. She had an uneasy feeling as though the Vicar's wife were walking about the house in her sad way, opening and shutting doors.

'Yes, we saw a great deal of Mrs. Fisk *senior*,' said the Vicar's wife. 'The Vicar was with her up to the End, you know.' The End had been in young Mrs. Fisk's bed and she didn't care to dwell on it. To see the Vicar's wife sit staring and dreaming there made her feel cold all over, as though the walls were glass. Mrs. Fisk saw a picture of the Vicar's wife and Euphemia composing Cottesby, laying him out on the kitchen table, gently and firmly closing that watchful eye. 'If she did lay out a corpse on my kitchen table,' thought Mrs. Fisk wrathfully, 'she'd never let me forgot it. She'd come in when I was rolling the pastry on it and look round in her watery way and say "Here's where we laid out dear Cottesby" . . . Her and her Mrs. Fisk senior!' Two more cups came up to be refilled; she lifted the teapot and found it disconcertingly light. She tilted the urn and found it was empty.

Here was a breakdown. Half way through tea Phyllis was to have come in for the urn and refilled it from a second kettle brought to the boil meanwhile on the kitchen fire. She stared into the urn, her jaw dropping; she went numb for a moment, then she was filled all over with a horror of death. 'There's a man dead on the stairs,' she kept thinking and 'They'll each want a third cup. I've no more tea for my visitors.' Her mind ran to and fro between these two facts like a mouse between the sides of a trap. Euphemia Wolley seemed to divine the crisis; she drained her cup hastily and handed it to her next door neighbour. '*If* you please,' said Euphemia. Here was Mrs. Hawke's, too, coming round. 'I never do drink more than two, but it's *so* good,' Mrs. Hawke smiled, sure of conferring a pleasure.

Mrs. Fisk felt sick. The whole tableful of cups seemed to take life and swim towards her, empty. 'A moment...' she said indistinctly. She got up, clutching the urn by each handle and walked from the room not too steadily.

Out in the hall she groped round for a chair and in quickly gathering darkness sat down with the urn on her knees. She was struggling, she never *had* fainted. She was in terror of dropping the urn yet dared not stoop to put it down. When the blackness cleared and she saw straight again she went, shaking all over, and stood at the top of the steps. The steps turned a corner, Cottesby sat just round that corner and couldn't be seen. She listened and there, just below her, dead silent, Cottesby seemed to be listening too. She could smell his clothes, earthy and sour. She thought of his greyish nose sticking slyly out through the banisters and that eye she had seen, filled with darkness.

All at once, finally, absolutely, she was afraid to go down. The hall clock, 'Mother's clock' – 'Mrs. Fisk' senior's – tick-tocked above her head, nagging at time. Behind the parlour door the voices petered out into silence; the Working Party was waiting for her, wondering what had become of her, anxiously listening.

Leaving the hall door ajar she fled, close in under the walls of the house. The first thin film of evening covered the sky; in the rickyard the pigeons fluttered and flopped: she fled through them, half mad from the outdoor silence, raising a cloud of dust and chaff. She rattled the gate, it was locked; she bundled her skirt up and climbed it. Stumbling, tottering on her high heels she fled up the valley; the cows looked after her placidly; further on, lambs fled to their mothers. Gates, wire, hedges themselves were no obstacle. The grey-green fields were uncomforting, the very colour of silence; the sky hung over the valley, from hill to hill, like a slack white sheet. The river slipped between reddening willows, sighing and shining. With the dread of her home behind her she fled up the empty valley. When she came in sight of the fields a mile from the house where her husband was working and saw men's figures dotted along the skyline, her voice, her wits, her sense of herself came back to her. Long before he could possibly hear she was calling out. . . .

'*William!* Oh, come down to me, William! There's a man on the stairs – he's sick – he's *dead* – I daren't go past him! William! I'm frightened – frightened – I don't dare stay in the house – all alone with him – all alone – *William!*'

She had forgotten the Working Party.

FOOTHOLD

'MORNING!' exclaimed Gerard, standing before the sideboard, napkin under his arm. 'Sleep well? There are kidneys here, haddock; if you prefer it, ham and boiled eggs – I don't *see* any boiled eggs but I suppose they are coming in – did you see Clara?'

Thomas came rather dazedly round the breakfast table.

'He's hardly awake,' said Janet. 'Don't shout at him, Gerard – Good morning, Thomas – let him sit down and think.'

'*Are* the boiled eggs——?' cried Gerard.

'Yes, of course they are. Can you possibly bear to wait?' she added, turning to Thomas. 'We are very virile at breakfast.'

Thomas smiled. He took out his horn-rimmed glasses, polished them, looked round the dining-room. Janet did things imaginatively; a subdued, not too buoyant prettiness had been superimposed on last night's sombre effect; a honey-coloured Italian table-cloth on the mahogany, vase of brown marigolds, breakfast-china about the age of the house with a red rim and scattered gold pimpernels. The firelight pleasantly jiggled, catching the glaze of dishes and coffee-pot, the copper feet of the 'sluggards' joy'. The square high room had, like Janet, a certain grace of proportion.

'I'm glad you don't have blue at breakfast,' said Thomas, unfolding his napkin. 'I do hate blue.'

'Did he see Clara?' asked Gerard, clattering the dish-lids. 'Do find out if he saw Clara!'

Janet was looking through a pile of letters. She took up each envelope, slit it open, glanced at the contents and slipped them inside again unread. This did not suggest indifference; the more she seemed to like the look of a letter the more quickly she put it away. She had put on shell-rimmed spectacles for reading, which completed a curious similarity between her face and Thomas's; both sensitive and untroubled, with the soft lines of easy living covering over the harder young lines of eagerness, self-distrust and a capacity for pain. When Gerard clamoured she raised her shoulders gently. 'Well, did you?' she said at last, without looking up from her letters.

'I'm afraid Clara's been encouraged away,' said Thomas. 'I specially left out some things I thought might intrigue her; a letter from Antonia, a daguerreotype of my grandmother I brought down to show you, rather a good new shirt – lavender-coloured. Then I lay awake some time waiting for her, but your beds are too comfortable. I had – disappointingly – the perfect night! Yet all through it I never quite forgot; it was like expecting a telephone call.'

'If you'd been half a man,' said Gerard, 'and Clara'd been half a ghost, you'd have come down this morning shaking all over with hair bright white, demanding to be sent to the first train.'

Janet, sitting tall and reposeful, swept her letters together with a movement and seemed faintly clouded. 'Well, I'm very glad Thomas isn't trying to go – tell me, why should Antonia's letters intrigue her? You complained they were rather dull. *I* find them dull, but then she isn't a woman's woman.'

'I just thought the signature ought to suggest an affinity. Names, you know. Meredith . . . Don't be discouraged, Gerard; I'm no sort of a test. I've slept in all sorts of places. There seems to be some sort of extra thick coating between me and anything other than fleshly.'

'*I've* never met her,' said Gerard, 'but then I'm a coarse man and Clara's essentially feminine. Perhaps something may happen this evening. Try going to bed earlier – it was half-past one when we were putting the lights out. Clara keeps early hours.'

'Have you noticed,' Janet said composedly, 'that one may discuss ghosts quite intelligently, but never any particular ghost without being facetious?'

' – Forgive my being so purely carnal,' exclaimed Thomas suddenly, 'but this is the most excellent marmalade. Not gelatinous, not slimy. I never get quite the right kind. Does your cook make it?'

He had noticed that here was 'a sensitiveness'. Thomas proceeded conversationally like the impeccable dentist with an infinitesimally fine instrument, choosing his area, tapping within it nearer and nearer, withdrawing at a suggestion before there had been time for a wince. He specialized in a particular kind of friendship with that eight-limbed, inscrutable, treacherous creature, the happily-married couple; adapting himself closely and lightly to the composite personality. An indifference to, an apparent unconsciousness of, life in some aspects armoured him against embarrassments. As Janet said, he would follow one into one's bedroom without noticing. Yet the too obvious 'tact', she said, *was* the literal word for his quality. Thomas was all finger-tips.

Janet slid her chair back noiselessly on the carpet and turned half round to face the fire. 'You're so nice and greedy,' she said, 'I do love having our food appreciated.'

'*I* appreciate it,' said Gerard. 'You know how I always hate staying away with people. I suppose I am absolutely smug. Now that we've come to this house I hate more than ever going up to the office.' He got up and stood, tall and broad, looking out of the window. Beyond, between the heavy fall of the curtains, showed the cold garden; the clipped shrubs like patterns in metal, the path going off in a formal perspective to the ascent of some balustraded steps. Beyond the terrace, a parade of trees on a not very remote skyline, the still, cold, evenly-clouded sky.

A few minutes afterwards he reluctantly left them. Janet and Thomas stood at the door and, as the car disappeared at the turn of the drive, Gerard waved goodbye with a backward scoop of the hand. Then they came in again to the fire and Thomas finished his coffee. He observed, 'The room seems a good deal smaller. Do you notice that rooms are adaptable?'

'I do feel the house has grown since we've been in it. The rooms seem to take so much longer to get across. I'd no idea we were buying such a large one. I wanted it because it was white, and late Georgian houses are unexigeant, but I promised myself – and everyone else – it was small.'

'Had you been counting on Clara, or didn't you know?'

'I was rather surprised. I met her coming out of your room about four o'clock one afternoon in November. Like an idiot I went downstairs and told Gerard.'

'Oh – why like an idiot?'

'He came dashing up, very excited – I suppose it was

rather exciting – and I came after him. We went into all the rooms, flinging the doors open as quietly and suddenly as we could; we even looked into the cupboards, though she is the last person one could imagine walking into a cupboard. The stupid thing was that I hadn't looked round to see which way she had gone. Gerard was perfectly certain there must be some catch about that chain of doors going through from my room to his and from his down the steps to the landing where there is a bathroom. He kept saying, "You go round one way and I'll go the other." While we'd been simply playing the fool I didn't mind, but when he began to be rational I began to be angry and – well, ashamed. I said: "If she's . . . not like us . . . you know perfectly well we can't corner her, and if she should be, we're being simply eccentric and rude." He said "Yes, that's all very well, but I'm not going to have that damned woman going in and out of my dressing-room," and I (thinking "Supposing she really is a damned woman?") said "Don't be so silly, she wouldn't be bothered – why should she?" Then the wind went out of our sails altogether. Gerard went downstairs whistling; we had tea rather irritably – didn't say very much and didn't look at each other. We didn't mention Clara again.'

'*Is* she often about?'

'Yes – no – I don't know . . . I really *don't* know, Thomas. I am wishing so much, you see, that I'd never begun her – let her in. Gerard takes things up so fearfully. I know last night when he took that second whisky and put more logs on we would be coming to Clara.'

'Ah,' said Thomas. 'Really. *That* was what you were waiting for. . . .'

' – The sun's trying to come out!' exclaimed Janet.

She got up and pushed the curtains further apart. 'In an hour or so when I've finished my house things we'll go round the garden. I do like having a garden you haven't seen. We're making two herbaceous borders down to the beech hedge away from the library window. I do think one needs perspective from a library window; it carries on the lines of the shelves.'

'Precious, I think,' said Thomas, 'distinctly precious.'

'Yes, I've always wanted to be . . . The papers are in the library.'

Thomas gathered from headlines and a half-column here and there that things were going on very much as he had expected. He felt remote from all this business of living; he was recently back from Spain. He took down Mabbe's *Celestina* and presently pottered out into the hall with his thumb in the book, to wait for Janet. In the hall, he looked at his own reflection in two or three pieces of walnut and noticed a Famille Rose bowl, certainly new, that they must have forgotten last night when they were showing him those other acquisitions. He decided, treading a zig-pattern across them carefully, that the grey and white marble squares of the floor were *good*; he would have bought the house on the strength of them alone. He liked also – Janet was doubtful about it – Gerard's treatment of the square-panelled doors, leaf-green in their moulded white frames in the smooth white wall. The stairs, through a double-doorway, had light coming down them from some landing window like the cold interior light in a Flemish picture. Janet, pausing half way down to say something to someone above, stood there as if painted, distinct and unreal.

Janet had brought awareness of her surroundings to such a degree that she could seem unconscious up to the very last fraction of time before seeing one, then give the effect with a look that said 'Still there?' of having had one a long time 'placed' in her mind. He could not imagine her startled, or even looking at anything for the first time. Thinking of Clara's rare vantage point, in November, up by his bedroom door, he said to himself, 'I'd give a good deal to have been Clara, that afternoon.'

'If you don't really mind coming out,' said Janet, 'I should put on an overcoat.' As he still stood there vaguely she took the book gently away from him and put it down on a table.

'If *I* had a ghost,' said Thomas as she helped him into an overcoat, 'she should be called "Celestina". I like that better than Clara.'

'If I have another daughter,' said Janet agreeably, 'she shall be called Celestina.'

They walked briskly through the garden in thin sunshine. Thomas, who knew a good deal about gardens, became more direct, clipped in his speech and technical. They walked several times up and down the new borders, then away through an arch in the hedge and up some steps to the terrace for a general survey. 'Of course,' she said, 'one works here within limitations. There's a character to be kept – you feel that? One would have had greater scope with an older house or a newer house. All the time there's a point of view to be respected. One can't cut clear away on lines of one's own like at Three Beeches; one more or less modifies. But it contents me absolutely.'

'You ought to regret that other garden?'

'I don't, somehow. Of course, the place was quite perfect; it had that kind of limitation – it was too much our own. We felt "through with it". I had some qualms about leaving, beforehand; I suppose chiefly moral – you know, we do spoil ourselves! – but afterwards, as far as regret was concerned, never a pang. Also, practically speaking, of course the house *was* getting too small for us. Children at school get into a larger way of living; when they come home for the holidays——'

'I suppose,' said Thomas distastefully, 'they do take up rather a lot of room.'

She looked at him, laughing. 'Hard and unsympathetic!'

'Hard and unsympathetic,' accepted Thomas complacently. 'I don't see where they come in. I don't see the point of them; I think they spoil things. Frankly, Janet, I don't understand about people's children and frankly I'd rather not . . . You and Gerard seem to slough your two off in a wonderful way. Do you miss them at all?'

'I suppose we——'

'*You*, you in the singular, thou?'

'I suppose,' said Janet, 'one lives two lives, two states of life. In terms of time, one may live them alternately, but really the rough ends of one phase of one life (always broken off with a certain amount of disturbance) seem to dovetail into the beginning of the next phase of that same life, perhaps months afterwards, so that there never seems to have been a gap. And the same with the other life, waiting the whole time. I suppose the two run parallel.'

'Never meeting,' said Thomas comfortably. 'You see I'm on one and your children are on the other and I want to be quite sure. Promise me: *never* meeting?'

'I don't think ever. But you may be wise, all the same, not to come in the holidays.'

They hesitated a moment or two longer on the terrace

as though there were more to be said and the place had
in some way connected itself with the subject, then came
down by the other steps and walked towards the dining-
room windows, rather consciously, as though someone
were looking out. She wore a leather coat, unbuttoned,
falling away from her full straight graceful figure, and a
lemon-and-apricot scarf flung round twice so that its
fringes hung down on her breast and its folds were
dinted in by the soft, still youthful line of her jaw.
Academically, Thomas thought her the most attractive
woman of his acquaintance: her bodily attraction was
modified and her charm increased by the domination of
her clear fastidious aloof mind over her body.

He saw her looking up at the house. 'I do certainly
like your house,' he said. 'You've inhabited it to a
degree I wouldn't have thought possible.'

'Thank you so much.'

'You're not – seriously, Janet – going to be worried
by Clara?'

'My dear, no! She does at least help fill the place.'

'You're not finding it empty?'

'Not the house, exactly. It's not . . .' They were
walking up and down under the windows. Some unusual
difficulty in her thoughts wrinkled her forehead and
hardened her face. 'You know what I was saying after
breakfast about the house having grown since we came
in, the rooms stretching? Well, it's not that, but my
life – *this* life – seems to have stretched somehow; there's
more room in it. Yet it isn't that I've more time – that
would be perfectly simple, I'd do more things. You
know how rather odious I've always been about *desœuvrées*
women; I've never been able to see how one's day could
fail to be full up, it fills itself. There's been the house,

the garden, friends, books, music, letters, the car, golf, when one felt like it, going up to town rather a lot. Well, I still have all these and there isn't a moment between them. Yet there's more and more room every day. I suppose it must be underneath.'

Thomas licked his upper lip thoughtfully. He suggested, 'Something spiritual, perhaps?' with detachment, diffidence and a certain respect.

'That's what anybody would say,' she agreed with equal detachment. 'It's just that I'm not comfortable; I always have been comfortable, so I don't like it.'

'It must be beastly,' said Thomas, concerned. 'You don't think it may just be perhaps a matter of not quite having settled down here?'

'Oh, I've settled down. Settled, I shouldn't be surprised to hear, for life. After all, Thomas, in eight years or so the children will, even from your point of view, really matter. They'll have all sorts of ideas and feelings; they'll be what's called "adult". There'll have to be a shifting of accents in this family.'

'When they come home for the holidays, what shall you do about Clara?'

'Nothing. Why should I? She won't matter. Not,' said Janet quickly, looking along the windows, 'that she matters particularly now.'

Thomas went up to his room about half-past three and, leaving the door open, changed his shoes thoughtfully after a walk. 'I cannot think,' he said to himself, 'why they keep dogs of that kind when exercising them ceases to be a matter of temperament and becomes a duty.' It was the only reflection possible upon the manner of living of Gerard and Janet. His nose and ears, nipped by the wind, thawed painfully in the even warmth of the house. Still with one shoe off he crossed the room on an impulse of sudden interest to study a print (some ruins in the heroic manner) and remained leaning before it in an attitude of reflection, his arms folded under him on the bow-fronted chest-of-drawers. The afternoon light came in through the big window, flooding him with security; he thought from the dogs to Gerard, from Gerard to Janet, whom he could hear moving about in her room with the door open, sliding a drawer softly open and shut. A pause in her movements – while she watched herself in the glass, perhaps, or simply stood looking critically about the room as he'd seen her do when she believed a room to be empty – then she came out, crossed her landing, came down the three steps to his passage and passed his door.

'Hullo, Janet,' he said, half turning round; she hesitated a moment, then went on down the passage. At the end there was a hanging-closet (he had blundered into it in mistake for the bathroom); he heard her click the door open and rustle about among the dresses. Still listening, he pulled open a small drawer under his elbow and searched at the back of it, under his ties, for the daguerreotype of his grandmother. Somehow he failed to hear her; she passed the door again silently; still with a hand at the back of the drawer he called out: 'Come in a moment, Janet, I've something to show you,' and turned full round quickly, but she had gone.

Sighing, he sat down and put on the other shoe. He washed his hands, flattened his hair with a brush, shook a clean handkerchief out of its folds with a movement of irritation and, taking up the daguerreotype, went out after her. 'Janet!' he said aggrievedly.

'Thomas?' said Janet's voice from the hall below.

'*Hul-lo!*'

'I've been shutting the dogs up – poor dears. We'll have tea in the library.' She came upstairs to meet him, drawing her gloves off and smiling.

'But you were in – I thought you – oh well, never mind . . .' He glanced involuntarily towards the door of her room; she looked after him.

'Yes, never mind,' she said. They smiled at each other queerly. She put her hand on his arm for a moment urgently, then with a little laugh went on upstairs past him and into her room. He had an instinct to follow her, a quick apprehension, but stood there rooted.

'Right-o; all clear,' she called after a second.

'Oh, right-o,' he answered, and went downstairs.

'By the way,' asked Thomas casually, stirring his tea, 'does one tell Gerard?'

'As you like, my dear. Don't you think, though, we might talk about *you* this evening? Yesterday we kept drawing on you for admiration and sympathy; you were too wonderful. We never asked you a thing, but what we should love really, what we are burning to do, is to hear about you in Spain.'

'I should love to talk about Spain after dinner. Before dinner I'm always a little doubtful about my experiences; they never seem quite so real as other people's; they're either un-solid or dingy. I don't get carried away by them myself, which is so essential . . . Just one thing: why is she so like you?'

'Oh! . . . did that strike *you*?'

'I never saw her properly, but it was the way you hold yourself. And her step – well, I've never been mistaken about a step before. And she looked in as she went by, over her shoulder, like you would.'

'Funny . . . So that was Clara. Nothing's ever like what one expected, is it?'

'No . . .' said Thomas, following a train of thought. 'She did perhaps seem eagerer and thinner. If I'd thought at all at the time (which I didn't) I'd have thought – "Something has occurred to Janet: what?" As it was, after she'd been by the second time I was cross because I thought you shouldn't be too busy to see me. What do you know about her – facts, I mean?'

'Very little. Her name occurs in some title-deeds. She was a Clara Skepworth. She married a Mr. Horace Algernon May and her father seems to have bought her the house as a wedding present. She had four children – they all survived her but none of them seems to have left descendants – and died a natural death, middle-aged, about 1850. There seems no reason to think she was not happy; she was not interesting. Contented women aren't.'

This Thomas deprecated. 'Isn't that arbitrary?'

'Perhaps,' agreed Janet, holding out a hand to the fire. 'You can defend Clara, I shan't . . . Why should I?'

'How do you know this Clara Skepworth – or May – is your Clara?'

'I just know,' said Janet, gently and a little wearily conclusive – a manner she must often have used with her children.

Thomas peppered a quarter of muffin with an air of giving it all his attention. He masked a keen intuition by not looking at Janet, who sat with her air of composed unconsciousness, perhaps a shade conscious of being considered. He had the sense here of a definite exclusion;

something was changing her. He had an intuition of some well he had half-divined in her having been tapped, of some reserve (which had given her that solidity) being drained away, of a certain sheathed and, till now, hypothetical faculty being used to exhaustion. He had guessed her capable of an intimacy, something disruptive, something to be driven up like a wedge, first blade-fine, between the controlled mind and the tempered, vivid emotions. It would not be a matter of friendship (the perfectness of his own with her proved it), she was civilized too deep down, the responses she made were too conscious; nor of love; she was perfectly mated (yet he believed her feeling for Gerard – so near to the casual eye, to the springs of her being – to be largely maternal and sensual).

In revulsion from the trend of his thoughts, he glanced at her: her comfortable beautiful body made the thing ludicrous. 'A peevish dead woman where we've failed,' he thought, 'it's absurd.' Gerard and he – he thought how much less humiliating for them both it would have been if she'd taken a lover.

'Gerard ought to be coming in soon.' Uneasy, like a watch-dog waking up at the end of a burglary, he glanced at the clock.

'Shall I put the muffins down by the fire again?'

'Why? Oh, no. He doesn't eat tea now, he thinks he is getting fat.'

'He's up to time usually, isn't he?'

'Yes – he's sure to be early this evening. I thought I heard the car then, but it was only the wind. It's coming up, isn't it?'

'Yes, lovely of it. Let it howl. (I like the third person imperative.)' He shrugged his folded arms up his chest luxuriously and slid down further into his chair. 'I like it after tea, it's so physical.'

'Isn't it?'

They listened, not for long in vain, for the sound of the car on the drive.

The drawing-room was in dark-yellow shadow with pools of light; Gerard and Janet were standing in front of the fire. Falling from Janet's arms above the elbows, transparent draperies hung down against the firelight. Her head was bent, with a line of light round the hair from a clump of electric candles on the wall above; she was looking into the fire, her arms stretched out, resting her finger-tips on the mantelpiece between the delicate china. Gerard, his fine back square and black to the room, bent with a creak of the shirt-front to kiss the inside of an elbow. Janet's fingers spread out, arching themselves on the mantelpiece as though she had found the chord she wanted on an invisible keyboard and were holding it down.

Thomas saw this from across the hall, through an open door, and came on in naturally. His sympathy was so perfect that they might have kissed in his presence; they both turned, smiling, and made room for him in front of the fire.

'Saturday tomorrow,' said Gerard, who smelt of verbena soap, 'then Sunday. Two days for me here. You've been here all day, Thomas. It doesn't seem fair.'

'I helped take the dogs for a walk,' said Thomas. 'It was muddy, we slid about and got ice-cold and couldn't talk at all because we kept whistling and whistling to the dogs till our mouths got too stiff. What a lot of virtue one acquires in the country by doing unnecessary things.

Being arduous, while there are six or eight people working full time to keep one alive in luxury.'

'Sorry,' said Janet. 'I didn't know you hated it. But I'm sure it was good for you.'

'I wish you wouldn't both imply,' said Thomas, 'that I don't know the meaning of work. On Monday, when I get back to town, I'm going to begin my book on monasteries.'

'What became of that poem about the Apocalypse?'

'I'm re-writing it,' said Thomas with dignity.

'You are the perfect mixture,' said Janet, 'of Francis Thompson and H. G. Wells.'

'There's a dark room in my flat where a man once did photography. In a year, when I'm thirty-five, I shall retire into it and be Proust, and then you will both be sorry.'

The butler appeared in the doorway.

'Dinner . . .' said Gerard.

When Janet left them, Gerard and Thomas looked at each other vaguely and wisely between four candles over a pile of fruit. The port completed its second circle. Thomas sipped, remained with lips compressed and, with an expression of inwardness, swallowed.

'Very ni-ice,' he said. '*Very* nice.'

'That's the one I was telling you – light of course.'

'I don't do with that heavy stuff.'

'No, you never could, could you . . . I'm putting on weight – notice?'

'Yes,' said Thomas placidly. 'Oh, well, it's time we began to. One can't fairly expect, my dear Gerard, to *look* ascetic.'

'Oh, look here, speak for yourself, you Londoner. I live pretty hard here – take a good deal of exercise. It would be beastly for Janet if one got to look too utterly gross.'

'Ever feel it?'

'M-m-m-m – no.'

Thomas sketched with his eyebrows an appeal for closer sincerity.

'Well, scarcely ever. Never more than is suitable.' He sent round the port. 'Had a good day barring the dogs? I daresay you talked a good deal; you made Janet talk well. She is, isn't she – dispassionately – what you'd call rather intelligent?'

'Yes – you proprietary vulgarian.'

'Thanks,' said Gerard. He cracked two walnuts between his palms and let the shells fall on to his plate with a clatter. 'I suppose she showed you everything out of doors? I shall show it you again tomorrow. Her ideas are quite different from mine, I mean about what we're going to do here. I shall have my innings tomorrow. She's keeping the men at those borders when I want them to get started on levelling the two new courts. We've only one now – I suppose she showed it you – which is ridiculous with Michael and Gill growing up. Well, I mean, it *is* ridiculous, isn't it?'

'Entirely,' said Thomas. 'Don't cramp the children's development; let them have five or six.'

'How you do hate our children,' said Gerard comfortably.

There ensued a mellowed silence of comprehension. Gerard, his elbows spread wide on the arms of his chair, stretched his legs further under the table and looked at the fire. Thomas pushed his chair sideways and crossed his legs still more comfortably. A log on the fire collapsed and went up in a gush of pale flame.

Thomas was startled to find Gerard's eyes fixed sharply upon him as though in surprise. He half thought that he must have spoken, then that Gerard had spoken. 'Yes?' he said.

'Nothing,' said Gerard, 'I didn't say anything, did I? As a matter of fact I was thinking – *did* you see anything of Clara?'

'If I were you I should drop Clara: I mean as a joke.'

There was nothing about Gerard's manner of one who has joked. He smiled grudgingly. 'I do work my jokes rather hard. I'm getting to see when their days are numbered by Janet's expression. As a matter of fact, I think *that's* one form of nerves with me; I feel it annoys Janet and I don't seem able to leave it alone . . . *You* don't think, seriously, there's anything in this thing?'

'I told you this morning I wasn't a test.'

'But aren't you?' insisted Gerard, with penetration. 'How about since this morning? How do you feel things are – generally?'

'She's an idea of Janet's.'

'Half your philosophers would tell me I was an idea of Janet's. I don't care what she is; the thing is, is she getting on Janet's nerves? You know Janet awfully well: do be honest.'

'It needs some thinking about. I'd never thought of Janet as a person who *had* nerves.'

'I'd like to know one way or the other,' said Gerard, 'before I start work on those courts.'

'My dear fellow – *leave here*?' Such an abysm of simplicity startled Thomas, who thought of his friends for convenience in terms of himself. *He* wouldn't leave here, once established, for anything short of a concrete discomfort, not for the menacing of all the Janets by all

the Claras. 'I've never seen Janet better,' he quickly
objected, 'looking nicer, more full of things generally.
You can't say the place doesn't suit her.'

'Oh yes, it suits her all right, I suppose. She's full
of – something. I suppose I'm conservative – inside,
which is so much worse – I didn't mind moving house, I
was keener than she was on coming here. I wanted this
place frightfully and I'm absolutely content now we've
got it. I've never regretted Three Beeches. But I
didn't reckon on one sort of change, and that seems to
have happened. I don't even know if it's something
minus or something plus. I think where I'm concerned,
minus. It's like losing a book in the move, knowing one
can't really have lost it, that it must have got into the
shelves somewhere, but not being able to trace it.'

'Beastly feeling,' said Thomas idly, 'till one remembers
having lent it to some devil who hasn't given it back.'

Gerard looked at him sharply, a look like a gasp. Then
his eyes dropped, his face relaxed from haggardness into
a set, heavy expression that held a mixture of pride and
resentment at his own impenetrability, his toughness.
Thomas knew the expression of old; when it appeared
in the course of an argument he was accustomed to drop
the argument with an, 'Oh well, I don't know. I daresay
you are right.' Gerard now raised his glass, frowned
expressively at it and put it down again. He said: 'I
must be fearfully fatuous; I always feel things are so
permanent.'

Thomas didn't know what to say; he liked Gerard
chiefly because he *was* fatuous.

'She's seeing too much of this ghost,' continued
Gerard. 'She wouldn't if things were all right with her.
I can't talk about delusions and doctors and things because

she's as healthy as I am, obviously, and rather saner. I daresay this thing's *here* all right; from the way you don't answer my question I gather you've been seeing it too.'

'To be exact,' said Thomas, 'somebody walked past my door this afternoon who turned out not to be Janet, though I'd have sworn at the time it was.'

'Tell Janet?'

'Yes.'

Gerard looked up for a moment and searched his face. 'Didn't you wonder,' he said, 'why she couldn't be natural about it? I remember she and you and I talking rot about ghosts at Three Beeches, and she said she'd love to induct one here. The first time she came down and told me about Clara I thought she thought it was fun. I suppose I was rather a hearty idiot; I rushed upstairs and started a kind of rat-hunt. I thought it amused her; when I found it didn't I had rather a shock . . . Things must be changing, or how can this Clara business have got a foothold? It *has* got a foothold – I worry a good bit when we're alone but we never discuss it, then directly somebody's here something tweaks me on to it and every time I try and be funny something gets worse . . . Oh, I don't know – I daresay I'm wrong.' Gerard dived for his napkin; he reappeared shame-faced. 'Wash this out,' he said, 'I've been talking through my hat. That's the effect of you, Thomas. It's not that you're so damned sympathetic, but you're so damned *un*sympathetic in such a provocative way.' He got up. 'Come on,' he said, 'let's come on out of here.'

Thomas got up unwillingly; he longed to define all this. Risking a failure in tact he put forward, 'What you're getting at is: all this is a matter of foothold?'

'Oh, I suppose so,' Gerard agreed non-committally. 'Let's wash that out, anyway. Do let's come on out of here.'

Thomas talked about Spain. 'I can't think why we don't go there,' cried Janet. 'We never seem to go anywhere; we don't travel enough. You seem so much completer and riper, Thomas, since you've seen Granada. Do go on.'

'Quite sure I don't bore you?' said Thomas, elated.

'Get on,' said Gerard impatiently. 'Don't stop and preen yourself. And, Janet, don't you keep on interrupting him. Let him get on.'

Thomas got on. He did require (as he'd told Janet) to gather momentum. Without, he was apt to be hampered by the intense, complacent modesty of the over-subjective; at the beginning, Spain refused to be detached from himself; he seemed to have made it. *Now* Spain imposed a control on him, selecting his language; words came less from him than through him, he heard them go by in a flow of ingenuous rapture.

Gerard and Janet were under the same domination. The three produced in each other, in talking, a curious sense of equality, of being equally related. Thomas concentrated a sporadic but powerful feeling for 'home' into these triangular contacts. He was an infrequent visitor, here as with other friends, but could produce when present a feeling of continuity, of uninterruptedness . . . It was here as though there had always been Thomas. The quiet room round them, secure from the whining wind, with its shadowy lacquer, its shades like great parchment cups pouring down light, the straight, almost palpable fall of heavy gold curtains to carpet, 'came together' in this peculiar intimacy as though it had lived a long time warm in their common memory. While he talked, it remained in suspension.

'O-oh,' sighed Janet and looked round, when he had finished, as though they had all come back from a journey.

'I suppose,' said Gerard, 'we are unenterprising. Are we?'

'A little,' conceded Thomas, still rather exalted, nursing one foot on a knee.

'Let's go abroad tomorrow!'

'You know,' exclaimed Janet, 'you know, Gerard, you'd simply hate it!' She made a gesture of limitation. 'We're rooted here.'

'Of course, there's one thing: if you hadn't both got this faculty for being rooted it wouldn't be the same thing to come and see you. I do hate "service-flat people"; I never know any.'

They all sighed, shifted their attitudes; sinking a little deeper into the big chairs. Thomas, aware almost with ecstasy of their three comfortable bodies, exclaimed: 'Would we ever really have known each other before there was this kind of chair? I've a theory that absolute comfort runs round the circle to the same point as asceticism. It wears the material veil pretty thin.'

Janet raised her arms, looked at them idly and dropped them again. 'What material veil?' she said foolishly.

Nobody answered.

'Janet's sleepy,' said Gerard, 'she can't keep awake unless she does all the talking herself. She's not one of your women who listen.'

'I wasn't sleepy till now. I think it's the wind. Listen to it.'

'Tomorrow, Janet, I'm going to show Thomas where those courts are to be. He says you didn't.'

'Thomas has no opinion about tennis courts; he'd agree with anyone. He really was intelligent about my borders.'

'Yes, I really was. You see, Gerard, tennis doesn't really affect me much. Pat-ball's my game.' Thomas lay back, looking through half-shut eyes at the wavering streaming flames. 'Clara's a dream,' he thought. 'Janet and I played at her. Gerard's a sick man.' He wanted to stretch sideways, touch Janet's bare arm and say to them both: 'There's just *this*, just this: weren't we all overwrought?'

Gerard, tenacity showing itself in his attitude, was sticking to something. He turned from one to the other eagerly. 'All the same,' he said, 'tennis courts or no tennis courts, why shouldn't we both, quite soon, go abroad?'

'Exactly,' said Thomas, encouraging.

'Because I don't want to,' said Janet. 'Just like that.'

'Oh . . . Tired?'

'Yes, tired-ish – with no disrespect to Thomas. I've had a wonderful day, but I *am* tired. Suppose it's the wind.'

'You said that before.'

She got up out of the depths of her chair, gathering up her draperies that slipped and clung to the cushions like cobwebs with perverse independence. 'Oh!' she cried. '*Sleepy!*' and flung her arms over her head.

'But you shatter our evening,' cried Thomas, looking up at her brilliance, then rising incredulous.

'Then you won't be too late,' she said heartlessly. 'Don't be too late!' She went across to the door like a sleepy cat. 'Good night, my dear Thomas.' After she closed the door they stood listening, though there was nothing to hear.

Their evening was not shattered, but it was cracked finely and irreparably. There was a false ring to it, never loud but an undertone. Gerard was uneasy; he got up after a minute or two and opened the door again. 'Don't you feel the room a bit hot?' he said. 'I'd open a window but the wind fidgets the curtains so. That's the only thing that gets on what nerves I have got, the sound of a curtain fidgeting; in and out, in and out, like somebody puffing and blowing.'

'Beastly,' said Thomas. 'I never open a window.' If he had been host he'd have invited Gerard to stop prowling and sit down, but one couldn't ask a man – even Gerard – to stop prowling about his own drawing-room when the prowling had just *that* 'tone'. So Thomas leant back rather exaggeratedly and sent up pacific smoke-wreaths.

'You look sleepy too,' said Gerard with some irritation. 'Shall we all go to bed?'

'Oh, just as you like, my dear fellow. I'll take up a book with me——'

' – No, don't let's,' said Gerard, and sat down abruptly.

The wind subsided during the next half-hour and silences, a kind of surprised stillness, spaced out their talk. Gerard fidgeted with the decanters; half way through a glass of whisky he got up again and stood undecided. 'Look here,' he said, 'there's something I forgot to ask Janet. Somebody's sent her a message and I must get the answer telephoned through tomorrow, first thing. I'll go up for a moment before she's asleep.'

'Do,' agreed Thomas, taking up *Vogue*.

Gerard, going out, hesitated rather portentously about shutting the drawing-room door and finally shut it. Thomas twitched an eyebrow but didn't look up from *Vogue*, which he went through intelligently from cover to cover. He remained looking for some time at a coloured advertisement of complexion soap at the end, then, as Gerard hadn't come back, got up to look for *Celestina*, where Janet had left it out in the hall. He crossed the hall soundlessly, avoiding the marble, stepping from rug to rug; with a hand put out for the *Celestina* he halted and stood still.

Gerard stood at the foot of the stairs, through the double doors, looking up, holding on to the banisters. Thomas looked at him, then in some confusion stepped back into the drawing-room. He had a shock; he wished he hadn't seen Gerard's face. 'What on earth was he listening for? . . . Why didn't he hear me? . . . I don't believe he's been up at all.' He took some more whisky and stood by the fire, waiting, his glass in his hand.

Quickly and noisily Gerard came in. 'She's asleep; it was no good.'

'Pity,' said Thomas, 'you ought to have gone up sooner.' They did not look at each other.

Thomas waited about – a social gesture purely, for he had the strongest possible feeling of not being wanted – while Gerard put out the downstair lights. Gerard wandered from one switch to another indeterminately, fumbling with wrong ones as though the whole lighting system were unfamiliar. Thomas couldn't make out if he were unwilling that either of them should go up, or whether he wanted Thomas to go up without him. 'I'll be going on up,' he said finally.

'Oh! Right you are.'

'I'll try not to wake Janet.'

'Oh, nothing wakes Janet – make as much noise as you like.'

He went up, his feet made a baffled, unreal sound on the smoothly carpeted stairs. The landing was – by some oversight – all in darkness. Away down the passage, firelight through his bedroom door came out across the carpet and up the wall. He watched – for Clara was somewhere, certainly – to see if anyone would step out across the bar of firelight. Nobody came. 'She may be in there,' he thought. Lovely to find her in there by the fire, like Janet.

Gerard turned out the last light in the hall and came groping up after him. 'Sorry!' he said. 'You'll find the switch of the landing outside Janet's door.' Thomas groped along the wall till he touched the door-panels. Left or right? – he didn't know, his fingers pattered over them softly.

'Oh, Clara,' came Janet's quiet voice from inside . . . 'I can't bear it. How could you bear it? The sickening loneliness . . . Listen, Clara. . . .'

He heard Gerard's breathing; Gerard there three steps below him, listening also.

'Damn you, Gerard,' said Thomas sharply and noisily. '*I* can't find this thing. I'm lost entirely. Why did you put those lights out?'

THE CASSOWARY

CRECY LODGE had stood empty for years; remote from the village it seemed to have been forgotten. The house hung doubtfully back from a by-road, obscured and almost smothered by limes; stucco gate-posts reared their depleted lions against a ground of evergreens. For Christmases, Crecy holly-branches had decorated the church; the theft was hallowed, yet those darkly cavernous or lividly-shuttered windows searching through the December garden still afforded spoilers an agreeable tremor. The chocolate gates were streaked a bright green from neglect and opened reluctantly, leaving green dust on the hands. In autumn when the new tenants arrived the drive was matted over with lime leaves that sent up a sodden odour, deadening the footsteps.

The house was under no discredit from any hint of the supernatural. It was over-large, and made no provision for modern living. Stuccoed and, but for the addition of a minaret on the east side, in the Gothic style, it was painted a pinkish grey and had a steep roof and pointed windows with low sills. It presented its worst aspect, the north, to an approach from the avenue, yet had a vulgar dignity, breadth and squareness sustaining its over-decoration with effect. From the west side ran out a long room with a rounded end and coloured windows that looked like an orangery but had been designed for a ballroom.

It did not seem likely that Mrs. Lampeter would give a ball for her daughters. The girls were elderly as girls, though young as spinsters; speaking socially, they were awkwardly placed in years. They were tall, 'rousses', each with a high-up stare (from the remarkable length of their fine necks) through pince-nez high on the chiselled noses. To this diffusion of their glances, the brilliantly blank look it gave them, turning to the light, they owed a slight air of vacuity, 'artistic', sometimes fumbling, generally elegant. In resemblance they varied between a Burne Jones and one of those Gallic drawings of English tourists. Their way of speaking – rapid, slurred, imperious, was such that one had always difficulty in understanding them and some diffidence in asking them to repeat what they had said. Their mother seemed attentive to them and was a little bowed.

The Vicar's wife was their first visitor; they were discovered by her reading and sewing, grouped, and received her cordially in a drawing-room blackly dominated by a mantelpiece like a cenotaph. This so put the room out of tone that the water-colours faded into the wall, the chrysanthemums were extinguished, and the chandelier catching up in some few drops all of the rainy light was alone vivid.

Mrs. Lampeter was supported in conversation by her elder daughter; they seemed travelled and interesting, subscribed to some weekly reviews and had lived near London. Mrs. Bonner, predisposed to enthusiasm, rapidly 'took to them'. The younger Miss Lampeter sat sideways with a polite appearance of attention; she leaned forward absently now and then to pick from the carpet some shreds of lime-leaf that had come in on Mrs. Bonner's heels. She was left-handed; Mrs. Bonner noticed upon the hand that advanced a black ring of enamel, discreet with pearls. She *did* look 'engaged'; rather distant.

'I understand,' Mrs. Lampeter said, 'there are not many young people about here?'

'Such a pity,' the caller nodded, resigned.

'Oh well,' cried the elder daughter surprisingly, 'we're accustomed to that!' The engaged Miss Lampeter, having come to an end of the lime leaves, resumed her embroidery with detachment.

'There are my two,' put out Mrs. Bonner, becomingly nonchalant, 'Robert and Margery. . . .'

A pale interest lit up the Lampeters. 'Couldn't they come to tea? Are they *quite* young?' exclaimed Miss Lampeter and, with eagerness, turned on the mother twin ovals of light from her pince-nez.

'They're away just at present. Margery's nineteen. Robert . . .' (she made a particular effort to sound matter-of-fact when she talked about Robert) 'he's seventeen.'

Miss Lampeter considered a moment or two. 'I expect we could play ping-pong . . . Can they play ping-pong?' she asked Mrs. Bonner.

Robert and Margery Bonner found themselves due for tea at the Lampeter's the first day of the holidays. Robert said blackly that this was the limit, and brooded. Margery wanted to know what they looked like and if they were rich. 'Are they pretty?' she asked. 'Who's she engaged to? Why doesn't she marry? I hate long engagements, they're governessy. And *what* made them come to that shattering house: are they under a cloud?'

'You'd better find out,' said Mrs. Bonner, who also genuinely wanted to know these things.

'Extraordinary to be that age. What can they think about?'

'Do be nice,' Mrs. Bonner said anxiously, seeing them off; she was never quite sure of her children. 'And remember to ask them about the holly for church.'

'I'll warn them that if they don't send some we'll steal it. We always have,' said the Vicar's daughter. To Robert she added, 'Hadn't Duckie better bring cricket-pads? They may be tigers at ping-pong.'

'*Funny!*' said Robert bitterly. He had been ravished from his laboratory, hands covered with chemical stains and smelling, he hoped, awful.

At tea in the dining-room Margery followed Phyllis's hand with her eyes; she guessed it pink-white, with dimples for knuckles and faintly freckled, but it fled everywhere with an independent shyness, passing dishes, gesturing, fluttering in a queer light way that seemed to be characteristic over hair around the exalted forehead. 'Wild as a deer,' thought Margery of the hand, which seemed apart from the rest of Phyllis's personality. 'If I'd a ring *there* I'd show it.' The Lampeter laughter, high in the roof of the mouth, was spontaneous and indefeasible. They emitted a ghostly childishness and seemed to be seated at table among a romping and laughter to which neither themselves nor their visitors contributed visibly. Their visitors stared like fishes, failing to understand them.

Robert's company manners were nice though sardonic. A clumsily built boy with an appearance of being continually bothered, he had a fixed interior-looking eye and hair that grew stiffly forward into a tuft when it should have grown back. His smile was so grudging that it became a compliment, suggesting to every comer her irresistibility, suggesting Robert was being amused in spite of himself. 'What a school-treat!' he would remark at intervals, looking critically up and down the laden table and helping himself to another slice of the Christmas cake that decorated the centre. He answered Mrs. and Miss Lampeter in a deep indulgent voice and was very much liked by them.

In a pause of her restless hospitality Phyllis Lampeter, sitting by Margery, looked at her vaguely as though she realized her guest had other needs than the purely material but could not think what to say to her. Across a gulf of ten years they stared at each other doubtingly. Margery envied other people's experience but felt a contempt for what they had probably made of it. She concealed her uncertainty how to behave in a grown-up world behind the directness of a successful woman of forty or a baby of four.

'Ripping ring!' she said clearly and suddenly, and pouncing on Phyllis's hand dragged it into the lamplight. 'Lucky . . .' she added, having assured herself as to the finger thus ornamented. Phyllis laughed sharply. She glanced across at her sister in what might have been either elation or dread apprehension of having been watched. Only Nathalie's rather flat quarter-face was, however, towards them; she was talking to Robert.

'Who are you going to marry?' said Margery.

Phyllis touched her pince-nez; they wobbled so she readjusted them, higher up on her nose. Nothing but flashes of light from them, shielding the look behind, came to Margery. 'I don't know whether he's alive,' said Phyllis and, mastering an impulse to turn away, looked at her visitor anxiously.

'Awful for you,' said Margery.

'It is, rather,' said Phyllis and half-laughed deprecatingly. A hand slid forward in sisterly pressure on
Phyllis's shoulder; above the top of her head Miss
Lampeter's pre-Raphaelite oval appeared and, high up,
another intelligent glimmer.

'Don't,' said Miss Lampeter softly, and to Margery's
embarrassment the sisters' hands touched.

'I wonder if this is how everyone behaved ten years
ago,' thought Margery. She got up with alacrity at a
suggestion from Miss Lampeter and they all went into
the ballroom to play ping-pong.

'What a wonderful house this is!' said Margery, sitting
down breathlessly on a sofa against the wall. The ballroom was lit by hanging lamps; it echoed disconcertingly
and had a forgotten smell. To and fro on the panelled
walls whisked the shadows of Phyllis Lampeter and
Robert, still running round the ping-pong table. Mrs.
Lampeter had gone away to sit by the drawing-room
fire, leaving what she evidently considered to be her
party of young people to play by themselves. Nathalie
Lampeter sat upright on the sofa, turning her long neck.
'We like it,' she said simply.

Her tall repose frightened Margery, who came out
with – 'I *have* been a clumsy idiot. I shan't be asked
here again.'

'Why not?' asked Miss Lampeter, with an obvious
resolution to understand her little visitor's point of view.
'I suppose it was a perfectly natural question.'

'Seeing the ring. . . .'

'Oh, quite. You couldn't be expected to guess that
there might be anything painful.'

'Awful of me,' said Margery, longing to know more. It came.

'My sister is engaged,' said Miss Lampeter, 'to a Mr. Melland, Paul Melland. He is a medical missionary and she saw him off to Central Africa two years ago. He used to write very regularly, but since a letter a year ago, a letter very much the same as usual saying that he was well, happy and interested in his work, nothing more has been heard of him. We have set inquiries on foot, even official inquiries, but he cannot be traced. Even his friends out there, his fellow-workers, know nothing of him. He left the station on an expedition up-country and cannot be traced.'

'It *sounds* like . . .' said Margery, shaking her head lugubriously.

'You would think so, wouldn't you?'

'Awfully sad for you all.'

'Awfully sad,' agreed Miss Lampeter, with a certain amount of detachment.

'Did *you* know him well?'

Miss Lampeter, leaning forward, was watching the couple at the ping-pong table intently. Her head turned to and fro. 'Know him? Very well, yes; intimately . . . We thought,' she said, 'that a change of interests for Phyllis . . . country life . . . young society. . . .'

'But he might come back?'

'Oh yes. I don't, personally, for a single moment cease to believe it.' Personally, Miss Lampeter seemed to believe a great deal. Behind this thin little trickle of information there was something stored up. 'Either she wants to make me feel there's something more up than appears to the eye,' thought Margery, 'or she thinks I'm a child or an idiot.' After another long, intense, yet blank look from Miss Lampeter's glasses she began to incline more and more to the former alternative. Nathalie ceased the tortoise movements of her head and, reflective, looking straight before her, sat like a statue. 'Paul was more to me than a brother,' she remarked in an aggrieved voice, and Margery believed that even this antique kind of bad form must have reached its limit.

'I am to regard this as confidential?'

'No,' said Miss Lampeter after a moment's consideration. 'No. Why? I believe it should save Phyllis pain and embarrassment if it were known generally. . . .'

Margery made the first of a series of efforts to 'save' Phyllis by telling Robert as soon as the door of Crecy Lodge, where the sisters had lingered politely, was shut behind them. Their path of lamplight cut off, they groped in total blackness down the slippery drive. Margery's narrative came in jerks and Robert received it flippantly.

' "I wish I were a cassowary",' he said promptly,

' "On the plains of Timbuctoo,
I should eat a Missionary,
Coat and hat and hymn-book too."

I don't blame the cassowary.' He was in high spirits but soon, his mind returning ahead of him to the laboratory, became abstracted.

'What a brute you are,' said Margery. 'That's a real tragedy. I don't call it funny at all.' She tripped over a root, clutched at Robert and began laughing, and she was still laughing, and breathless from impatience to be home and tell somebody else, when they overtook Mrs. Bonner in Vicarage Lane.

'But there's *nothing* funny about a missionary,' said Mrs. Bonner pained. 'He is very brave and splendid. It is *silly* of you, Robert. You *are* silly . . .' She laughed despairingly and wiped her eyes . . . there was something irresistibly witty and winning in Robert's poem about the cassowary. '*Preparatory* school humour!' said Mrs. Bonner scornfully, squeezing Robert's arm. 'Those unfortunate women! I wonder whether there is anything one could do. . . .'

There seemed nothing, except to surround the Miss Lampeters with an atmosphere of solicitude, which must be very bright, and to encourage forgetfulness. People in a nervous over-anxiety to do this often complained that whenever a Lampeter entered a room some outside power would twist round the most ordinary conversation in the direction of Central Africa, disappearances, or sudden and fearful death. In spite of this Phyllis Lampeter became in demand, flourished visibly and began to take on a satisfied matronly little air of having made her market. Mr. Melland, taboo but intensely vital, accompanied her everywhere; it was like meeting a married couple to whom the sister, her office of protector and showman declining, became an awkward and often superfluous third. The more Phyllis came in evidence with her Pot of Basil the more the '*doutre-Manche*' in Nathalie's gait and attitudes became accentuated.

Margery, however, did not care for widows; full of a spirit of opposition she began a cult of Nathalie, who helped her with the Girl Guides. Miss Lampeter was learning to moderate her first estranging effusiveness and to alternate less clumsily between rigidity and unreserve. She could not, however, cure herself of a frequent use of the diminutive, and a 'little Margery', winsome, bright, spontaneous and unknown at the Vicarage, became *persona grata* at Crecy Lodge. The uneasy house grew familiar to Margery, the loud shutting of the heavily-moulded doors, the cold limey breath from the passages, the sheen along empty rooms where one wandered of paint and marble in the immoderate glare from the windows, and, most of all in the rooms they inhabited, a suggestion about the general arrangements of being provisional; a kind of encamped and temporary expression about the furniture, the fall of the draperies, the pictures and ornaments, choice but too thinly disposed. By an almost over-discretion in the arrangement of the drawing-room each member of the family seemed to have striven and failed to impose on the others a feeling of permanence she herself did not possess. The harmony of those evenings Margery passed with the Lampeters seemed to her, looking back afterwards, to have been upheld intact, like a ball of glass upon a fountain, by a perpetual jet of effort. Evening on evening spent in Crecy lamp and fire-light could never assure her that at any time, twelve hours after, they might not have stolen away, and that only vast unlit chandelier would be left there dripping iridescently over an empty floor.

Margery, upon whom country evenings, mud, seclusion and Robert's absence soon began to pall, left home about the middle of February on a round of visits to her school-friends. She remained some weeks in London, went to theatres, shingled her hair and received a proposal of marriage. She was surprised and a good deal sobered by her inability to accept the young man, a friend's brother, who appeared to her in all ways suitable. She forgot the Lampeters, first deliberately and then with such ease and naturalness that when she did endeavour to remember them they returned reluctantly, very pale and almost indistinguishable. When she came home again, older, tenderer and more conscious, she avoided Crecy Lodge from some kind of shame.

In March, on a pale gusty day, she once more pushed open the chocolate gate reluctantly and, letting it swing behind her, listened to the wind that tore the lime trees and reflected on life's desolating continuity. Following the bend of the avenue she became exposed to the black stare of the windows, and in spite of another twinge of distaste and nervousness had to go forward. Having tugged the bell perfunctorily she walked unannounced, as she was privileged to do, into the arched hall and shouted for Nathalie and Phyllis. All round the doors were a little ajar, but nobody moved or answered. In pauses of the wind she should have been able to hear a fire rustle, the leaves of a book turn over or Nathalie's work-box creak, but it seemed for once as though the restless house were asleep.

'It's happened!' she thought in a flash, and, repeating this to herself without knowing at all what she meant, pushed through a swing door and went hurriedly down the passage into the ballroom. 'If they're not here,' she thought, 'they will really be gone.' But Miss Lampeter *was* there, in hat and furs, standing in the harlequin light of a window-embrasure and looking out steadfastly through a pane of blue glass. She knew Margery's step, and quickly, without turning, exclaimed: 'Paul's come back!'

Margery shut the door after her cautiously. 'Goodness!' she whispered.

'I hope,' said Miss Lampeter, 'I didn't startle you?'

'*You* must be startled.'

'N-no,' said Miss Lampeter slowly, with a kind of luxurious hesitation. 'Not startled . . . He's in London.'

'When, when . . . ?'

'We heard last night. Not a word before, not a rumour. Letters miscarried——'

'Phyllis——'

'We've had a terrible time with Phyllis; she wants to go up to London!'

'Naturally!'

'She can't,' said Miss Lampeter sharply. 'It would be hard on Paul, he's been ill. It wouldn't *do*. . . .'

'But he'll want her,' said Margery angrily.

Miss Lampeter shook her head violently, flashing her glasses. 'It wouldn't do,' she repeated; 'you don't understand. We've had a most terrible time with her. I have to think for both of them. Mother is upset.'

'Altogether a very nice home-coming – Nathalie, don't be an ass!' Margery, coming up awkwardly, put an arm round her friend, who trembled all over as though she were going to cry.

'It's so difficult, it's too difficult. Nobody understands. I'm distracted, you see,' said Nathalie, and looked at Margery reproachfully. 'You see,' she added, '*I* must go to London. . . .'

'I don't see. . . .'

'I can't explain. Yet I shall have to explain . . . I could almost wish sometimes he hadn't come home.'

'Must anyone go to London? Can't he come——'

'*I* must see Paul.'

A swirl round the house, a door swinging, the rattle of windows along the north side of the room made Margery feel that someone else must be coming distractedly down the passage. She looked about in alarm with some idea of getting out through a window and a horrible sense of complicity.

'Anyone would say,' said Miss Lampeter, 'that I'd broken Phyllis's heart. But I can't let there be a mistake, can I? I've got to see Paul. And they none of them want me too.' She stood knitting her ringless fingers together, looking down at them in despair.

'You see, things are so difficult – life in a family. We've never spoken of this among ourselves. None of us liked to begin. Phyllis is everything to me – everything *else*. Love's so embarrassing, isn't it? I'm sure we've all felt, this last year, it was the only solution, his not coming back . . . Scenes are so dreadful; we've never had scenes in our family.'

'When's your train?'

'The twelve nine. Now let me go!' said Miss Lampeter sharply, freeing herself with a movement from some imaginary constraint. Margery, ashamed of this tempest and of something unknown in herself that was answering it, stood away from her, looking up at the coloured squares of sky.

'There's Phyllis,' said Margery suddenly. '*Now* what shall you do?'

Nathalie made a sudden assault on the latch, the french windows were snatched by a gust and flung violently back against the wall of the house. She stumbled out into the wind and went slanting against it, her skirts whipped round her legs, across the garden to the avenue trees. Margery ran out after her with her umbrella and purse. 'Tell Phyllis!' Miss Lampeter threw back over her shoulder.

Phyllis, looking across the garden, had appeared in

the window. 'Gone, I suppose?' said Phyllis, vague,
weary, a shade depressed.

'Do you mind?'

Phyllis took no notice; she said, 'I suppose I had better
tell Mother.' She blinked, having appeared for the first
time without her glasses; her eyes, large, bright, timid
and inexpressive, were ringed with gold lashes. 'She isn't
half dressed,' said Phyllis plaintively. 'She's taken the
wrong umbrella. I don't know what Paul will think. I've
had the most terrible time with her, she's so excited.'

Phyllis shut and latched the ballroom window and
took Margery's arm: they went up the passage together
into the drawing-room. Here, asking Margery to poke
the fire for her, she sat down in her usual chair and
took up her work. She sucked in her underlip, her chin
was drawn plaintively back like a child's. Her attitude
drooped.

'What a wind,' said Margery, listening nervously.

'I don't suppose,' said Phyllis, watching her needle,
'you know what to make of us all. I'm afraid all this
is rather embarrassing. As a matter of fact it is embarrassing for all of us. In a kind of way, of course, we've been
unsettled for years, but we were getting used to that and
now all this has come and upset us completely. Of course,
one is *deeply* thankful, but one can't help feeling that it
would have been simpler if he hadn't come back. Of
course I need not tell you, Margery, that all this is
strictly confidential. We have never spoken of this
among ourselves. You see, we all mean so much to each
other, Mother and Nathalie and I, that discussion is
quite impossible. We should never have felt the same.'

'Nathalie's cared for Paul ever since we knew him.
Her feelings are very strong. I never knew why they

didn't marry: I don't really know Paul well enough in a way to ask. Anyhow, then I grew up and I suppose' – said Phyllis indifferently, looking round for the scissors – 'I was the more attractive. Paul asked me and Nathalie was so sweet about our engagement, but of course she knew I knew about *her* and it was most embarrassing. It must have been difficult for her, for the engagement has lasted for years; Paul couldn't afford to marry and it seemed almost a good thing when he went out to Central Africa. We corresponded quite regularly till one day I got a letter saying he was in love with Nathalie and asking me to release him. I was very much upset, naturally, and didn't know what to say, for I always felt Paul doesn't know his own mind very distinctly, and I didn't see really why he shouldn't marry me when he'd had the best years of my life and we'd been engaged so long. While I was still wondering what to do, his letters stopped, and later on we heard bad news from the Mission station. Then there didn't seem then any harm in my going on as I'd been before. You can't release a dead person, and I was so much accustomed to being engaged, you see. Nathalie was sweet to me and always talked of Paul as mine and let me be a kind of widow, but I always felt she meant to have him if he ever came back, and of course I fully intended, if that *should* happen, to give him up. Mother knew of it all, of course, and it was most distressing for her: she never speaks of it.'

Phyllis sighing, smoothed out her embroidery and remained looking pensively down at her ring. 'I must say,' she said plaintively, 'I don't think she's treated me fairly, do you, Margery? *I* ought to have gone up to London. After all, I am still engaged to Paul. I'm accustomed to being engaged.'

'She was in a hurry – naturally.'

'I don't think it's at all natural,' said Phyllis, working herself up. 'I call it highly unnatural. She's my own sister. And she has nothing to say to Paul that she can at all properly say.'

'Wouldn't you put that right?'

'No, I won't,' said Phyllis, high-pitched. 'I don't see why I should. I won't go back to nothing at all after being a kind of widow. It's preposterous.'

Rigid with indignation she blinked her gold lashes. 'Nathalie's accustomed to home life,' she said, and looked indignantly round the drawing-room.

Some memory in the room compelled her and she resumed her remote expression, the air, which had become part of herself, of pleasurable uncertainty, as of one expecting momentarily to be called away. That she was to be denuded of this, that her encampment in the bare house was to become a permanency, appalled Margery, who said violently:

'He should never have come back!'

'Oh, *Margery*,' smiled the engaged girl – the ringed hand fluttered the hair round what seemed now a beaming, a bridal forehead – 'what a *ridiculous* thing to say!'

But Nathalie, having got her telegram off, now sat washed smooth by the speed of that friendly and eager train. It was an hour afterwards, Margery learnt, that in the crowd on Paddington platform Paul and Nathalie kissed – decorously, like husband and wife for a week parted.

'And I left my umbrella in the train!' she exclaimed afterwards. ' – Oh, Paul, Phyllis's umbrella!'

'That is too bad,' said Paul, perfunctory.

TELLING

T E R R Y looked up; Josephine lay still. He felt
shy, embarrassed all at once at the idea of anyone
coming here. His brain was ticking like a watch:
he looked up warily.

But there was nobody. Outside the high cold walls,
beyond the ragged arch of the chapel, delphiniums
crowded in sunshine – straining with brightness, burning each other up – bars of colour that, while one watched
them, seemed to turn round slowly. But there was
nobody there.

The chapel was a ruin, roofed by daylight, floored with
lawn. In a corner the gardener had tipped out a heap
of cut grass from the lawn-mower. The daisy-heads
wilted, the cut grass smelt stuffy and sweet. Everywhere,
cigarette-ends, scattered last night by the couples who'd
come here to kiss. First the dance, thought Terry, then
this: the servants will never get straight. The cigarette-
ends would lie here for days, till after the rain, and go
brown and rotten.

Then he noticed a charred cigarette stump in Josephine's hair. The short wavy ends of her hair fell back –
still in lines of perfection – from temples and ears; by
her left ear the charred stump showed through. For
that, he thought, she would never forgive him; fastidious-
ness was her sensibility, always tormented. ('If you must
know,' she had said, 'well, you've got dirty nails, haven't

you? Look.') He bent down and picked the cigarette-
end out of her hair; the fine ends fluttered under his
breath. As he threw it away, he noticed his nails were
still dirty. His hands were stained now – naturally – but
his nails must have been dirty before. Had she noticed
again?

But had she, perhaps, for a moment been proud of
him? Had she had just a glimpse of the something he'd
told her about? He wanted to ask her: 'What do you feel
now? Do you believe in me?' He felt sure of himself,
certain, justified. For nobody else would have done
this to Josephine.

Himself they had all – always – deprecated. He felt a
shrug in this attitude, a thinly disguised kind of hope-
lessness. 'Oh, *Terry* . . .' they'd say, and break off.
He was no good: he couldn't even put up a tennis-net.
He never could see properly (whisky helped that at first,
then it didn't), his hands wouldn't serve him, things
he wanted them to hold slipped away from them. He
was no good; the younger ones laughed at him till they,
like their brothers and sisters, grew up and were schooled
into bitter kindliness. Again and again he'd been sent
back to them all (and repetition never blunted the bleak
edge of these home-comings) from school, from Cam-
bridge, now – a month ago – from Ceylon. 'The bad
penny!' he would remark, very jocular. 'If I could just
think things out,' he had tried to explain to his father,
'I know I could do *something*.' And once he had said to
Josephine: 'I know there is Something I could do.'

'And they will know now,' he said, looking round
(for the strange new pleasure of clearly and sharply
seeing) from Josephine's face to her stained breast (her
heavy blue beads slipped sideways over her shoulder and

coiled on the grass – touched, surrounded now by the unhesitant trickle); from her breast up the walls to their top, the top crumbling, the tufts of valerian trembling against the sky. It was as though the dark-paned window through which he had so long looked out swung open suddenly. He saw (clear as the walls and the sky) Right and Wrong, the old childish fixities. I have done right, he thought (but his brain was still tickling). *She ought not to live* with this flaw in her. Josephine ought not to live, she had to die.

All night he had thought this out, walking alone in the shrubberies, helped by the dance-music, dodging the others. His mind had been kindled, like a dull coal suddenly blazing. He was not angry; he kept saying: 'I must not be angry, I must be just.' He was in a blaze (it seemed to himself) of justice. The couples who came face to face with him down the paths started away. Someone spoke of a minor prophet, someone breathed 'Caliban.' . . . He kept saying: 'That flaw right through her. She damages truth. She kills souls; she's killed mine.' So he had come to see, before morning, his purpose as God's purpose.

She had laughed, you see. She had been pretending. There was a tender and lovely thing he kept hidden, a spark in him; she had touched it and made it the whole of him, made him a man. She had said: 'Yes, I believe, Terry. I understand.' That had been everything. He had thrown off the old dull armour . . . Then she had laughed.

Then he had understood what other men meant when they spoke of her. He had seen at once what he was meant to do. 'This is for me,' he said. 'No one but I can do it.'

All night he walked alone in the garden. Then he watched the french windows and when they were open again stepped in quickly and took down the African knife from the dining-room wall. He had always wanted that African knife. Then he had gone upstairs (remembering, on the way, all those meetings with Josephine, shaving, tying of ties), shaved, changed into flannels, put the knife into his blazer pocket (it was too long, more than an inch of the blade came out through the inside lining) and sat on his window-sill, watching sunlight brighten and broaden from a yellow agitation behind the trees into swathes of colour across the lawn. He did not think; his mind was like somebody singing, somebody able to sing.

And, later, it had all been arranged for him. He fell into, had his part in, some kind of design. Josephine had come down in her pleated white dress (when she turned the pleats whirled). He had said, 'Come out!' and she gave that light distant look, still with a laugh at the back of it, and said, 'Oh – right-o, little Terry.' And she had walked down the garden ahead of him, past the delphiniums into the chapel. Here, to make justice perfect, he had asked once more: '*Do* you believe in me?' She had laughed again.

She lay now with her feet and body in sunshine (the sun was just high enough), her arms flung out wide at him, desperately, generously: her head rolling sideways in shadow on the enclosed, silky grass. On her face was a dazzled look (eyes half closed, lips drawn back), an expression almost of diffidence. Her blood quietly soaked through the grass, sinking through to the roots of it.

He crouched a moment and, touching her eyelids –

still warm – tried to shut her eyes. But he didn't know how. Then he got up and wiped the blade of the African knife with a handful of grass, then scattered the handful away. All the time he was listening; he felt shy, embarrassed at the thought of anyone finding him here. And his brain, like a watch, was still ticking.

On his way to the house he stooped down and dipped his hands in the garden tank. Someone might scream; he felt embarrassed at the thought of somebody screaming. The red curled away through the water and melted.

He stepped in at the morning-room window. The blinds were half down – he stooped his head to avoid them – and the room was in dark-yellow shadow. (He had waited here for them all to come in, that afternoon he arrived back from Ceylon.) The smell of pinks came in, and two or three blue-bottles bumbled and bounced on the ceiling. His sister Catherine sat with her back to him, playing the piano. (He had heard her as he came up the path.) He looked at her pink pointed elbows – she was playing a waltz and the music ran through them in jerky ripples.

'Hullo, Catherine,' he said, and listened in admiration. So his new voice sounded like this!

'Hullo, Terry.' She went on playing, worrying at the waltz. She had an anxious, methodical mind, but loved gossip. He thought: Here is a bit of gossip for you – Josephine's down in the chapel, covered with blood. Her dress is spoilt, but I think her blue beads are all right. I should go and see.

'I say, Catherine——'

'Oh, Terry, they're putting the furniture back in the drawing-room. I wish you'd go and help. It's getting

those big sofas through the door . . . and the cabinets.'
She laughed: 'I'm just putting the music away,' and
went on playing.

He thought: I don't suppose she'll be able to marry
now. No one will marry her. He said: 'Do you know
where Josephine is?'

'No, I haven't' – rum-tum-tum, rum-tum-*tum* – 'the
slightest idea. Go on, Terry.'

He thought: She never liked Josephine. He went
away.

He stood in the door of the drawing-room. His
brothers and Beatrice were punting the big armchairs,
chintz-skirted, over the waxy floor. They all felt him
there: for as long as possible didn't notice him. Charles –
fifteen, with his pink scrubbed ears – considered a
moment, shoving against the cabinet, thought it was
rather a shame, turned with an honest, kindly look of
distaste, said, 'Come on, Terry.' He can't go back to
school now, thought Terry, can't go anywhere, really:
wonder what they'll do with him – send him out to the
Colonies? Charles had perfect manners: square, bluff,
perfect. He never thought about anybody, never felt
anybody – just classified them. Josephine was 'a girl
staying in the house', 'a friend of my sisters'. He would
think at once (in a moment when Terry had told him),
'A girl staying in the house . . . it's . . . well, I mean, if
it hadn't been *a girl staying in the house*. . . .'

Terry went over to him; they pushed the cabinet.
But Terry pushed too hard, crooked; the further corner
grated against the wall. 'Oh, I say, we've scratched the
paint,' said Charles. And indeed they had; on the wall
was a grey scar. Charles went scarlet: he hated things
to be done badly. It was nice of him to say: '*We've*

scratched the paint.' Would he say later: 'We've killed Josephine'?

'I think perhaps you'd better help with the sofas,' said Charles civilly.

'You should have seen the blood on my hands just now,' said Terry.

'Bad luck!' Charles said quickly and went away.

Beatrice, Josephine's friend, stood with her elbows on the mantelpiece looking at herself in the glass above. Last night a man had kissed her down in the chapel (Terry had watched them). This must seem to Beatrice to be written all over her face – what else could she be looking at? Her eyes in the looking-glass were dark, beseeching. As she saw Terry come up behind her she frowned angrily and turned away.

'I say, Beatrice, do you know what happened down in the chapel?'

'Does it interest you?' She stooped quickly and pulled down the sofa loose-cover where it had 'runkled' up, as though the sofa legs were indecent.

'Beatrice, what would you do if I'd killed somebody?'

'Laugh,' said she, wearily.

'If I'd killed a woman?'

'Laugh harder. Do you know any women?'

She was a lovely thing, really: he'd ruined her, he supposed. He was all in a panic. 'Beatrice, swear you won't go down to the chapel.' Because she might, well – of course she'd go down: as soon as she was alone and they didn't notice she'd go creeping down to the chapel. It had been *that* kind of kiss.

'Oh, be quiet about that old chapel!' Already he'd spoilt last night for her. How she hated him! He looked round for John. John had gone away.

On the hall table were two letters, come by the second post, waiting for Josephine. No one, he thought, ought to read them – he must protect Josephine; he took them up and slipped them into his pocket.

'I say,' called John from the stairs, 'what are you doing with those letters?' John didn't mean to be sharp but they had taken each other unawares. They none of them wanted Terry to *feel* how his movements were sneaking movements; when they met him creeping about by himself they would either ignore him or say: 'Where are *you* off to?' jocosely and loudly, to hide the fact of their knowing he didn't know. John was Terry's elder brother, but hated to sound like one. But he couldn't help knowing those letters were for Josephine, and Josephine was 'staying in the house'.

'I'm taking them for Josephine.'

'Know where she is?'

'Yes, in the chapel . . . I killed her there.'

But John – hating this business with Terry – had turned away. Terry followed him upstairs, repeating: 'I killed her there, John . . . John, I've killed Josephine in the chapel.' John hurried ahead, not listening, not turning round. 'Oh, yes,' he called over his shoulder. 'Right you are, take them along.' He disappeared into the smoking-room, banging the door. It had been John's idea that, from the day after Terry's return from Ceylon, the sideboard cupboard in the dining-room should be kept locked up. But he'd never said anything; oh no. What interest could the sideboard cupboard have for a brother of his? he pretended to think.

Oh yes, thought Terry, you're a fine man with a muscular back, but you couldn't have done what I've done. There had, after all, been Something in Terry.

He *was* abler than John (they'd soon know). John had never kissed Josephine.

Terry sat down on the stairs saying: 'Josephine, Josephine!' He sat there gripping a baluster, shaking with exaltation.

The study door-panels had always looked solemn; they bulged with solemnity. Terry had to get past to his father; he chose the top left-hand panel to tap on. The patient voice said: 'Come in!'

Here and now, thought Terry. He had a great audience; he looked at the books round the dark walls and thought of all those thinkers. His father jerked up a contracted, strained look at him. Terry felt that hacking with his news into this silence was like hacking into a great, grave chest. The desk was a havoc of papers.

'What exactly do you want?' said his father, rubbing the edge of the desk.

Terry stood there silently: everything ebbed 'I want,' he said at last, 'to talk about my future.'

His father sighed and slid a hand forward, rumpling the papers. 'I suppose, Terry,' he said as gently as possible, 'you really *have* got a future?' Then he reproached himself. 'Well, sit down a minute . . . I'll just. . . .'

Terry sat down. The clock on the mantelpiece echoed the ticking in his brain He waited.

'Yes?' said his father.

'Well, there must be some kind of future for me, mustn't there?'

'Oh, certainly. . . .'

'Look here, father, I have something to show you. That African knife——'

'What about it?'

'That African knife. It's here. I've got it to show you.'

'What about it?'

'Just wait a minute.' He put a hand into either pocket: his father waited.

'It *was* here – I did have it. I brought it to show you. I must have it somewhere – that African knife.'

But it wasn't there, he hadn't got it; he had lost it; left it, dropped it – on the grass, by the tank, anywhere. He remembered wiping it . . . Then?

Now his support was all gone; he was terrified now; he wept.

'I've lost it,' he quavered, 'I've lost it.'

'What do you mean?' said his father, sitting blankly there like a tombstone, with his white, square face.

'What are you trying to tell me?'

'Nothing,' said Terry, weeping and shaking. 'Nothing, nothing, nothing.'

MRS. MOYSEY

MRS. MOYSEY'S nephew came home from Japan, suddenly, and paid her a long visit. She was very much touched by his liking to be with her, though fluttered, because Mr. Moysey had now been dead some time and her household had got out of a gentleman's ways. Leslie, however, was accommodating and kind and made every allowance; she implored him not to be shy about mentioning things and he very soon wasn't. He didn't want to be entertained, he sat most of the day in the dining-room bow-window, leaning back smoking and watching the people go up and down High Street. Sometimes he would ring the bell for the parlourmaid, or call to his aunt, to ask who somebody was. They were delighted to tell him. The people who interested Leslie most were ladies, young-middle-aged married ladies with nice figures.

Also, Mrs. Moysey had been fluttered by Leslie's arrival because she (and the household) had got into little ways of her own which seemed silly at once when one thought of anyone watching them. She went out either early, before everyone else was about, or late when most people were in again, coming home always with such an armful of parcels that she had to steady the top with her chin while she got out her latchkey. Then she would push the door gingerly back and slip in round it. Someone wittily said she looked like Christmas

Eve every day. She spent most of the day in her bed-room; a room, very cosily furnished, overlooking the gardens behind the street. If anyone knocked she'd say 'Who's there?' in a muffled and rather fierce voice. She never said 'Come in', because she did not mean come in. If one persisted, after a minute or two she'd come out herself, rather flushed. Leslie, having experienced this, gave up knocking. He was full of delicacy. When his aunt came down for the evening, with her pale fluffy hair whipped up beautifully on the top of her head like confectioner's cream, a écru lace blouse and a string of green shells brought round twice and knotted over the bosom, he'd cry 'Auntie!' languidly rapturous, swing his feet off the rung of a chair and get up. He got up just slowly enough for her to feel every time how polished it was of Leslie to get up at all. In the evenings they were companionable, very cosy together, in spite of a habit of Mrs. Moysey's of not sitting anywhere long or of fully relaxing, as though she were trying a new kind of stays that were not a success. At ten o'clock the parlourmaid brought in the decanters, Mrs. Moysey would say, 'Well nightie-night I suppose,' and get finally up, between regret and alacrity.

Everybody in town knew Mrs. Moysey and liked her, in spite of what was called 'the little failing'. Nobody specified what the little failing was; there existed an understanding. Yet it did seem curious that the parcels one saw her slip home with in the cold morning or in the evening dusk might be round, square or diamond-shaped, hard or bulgy, but were never cylindrical. And no one had ever seen her go into or come out of a – well, one wouldn't like to say what. But so flushed, so abrupt, so secretive – there wasn't a doubt.

Her friends, when first Leslie, exotic and waxlike, began to be displayed in the bow-window, were sympathetic and interested. There would be fewer temptations for poor Mrs. Moysey now she was having young people about the house. Not long afterwards she gave a party and asked all the ladies Leslie admired most. They came, the drawing-room was unaccustomedly brilliant, they tinkled like lustres. But Leslie liked the ladies' conversation less than their figures. Perhaps he could have dealt with them better singly, at all events he went into a kind of stupor, blinked, and from looking at each of them not at all nicely passed to not looking at any of them at all. Before the end of tea he got up and went out; they could hear him moving glasses about in the dining-room and doing things with a syphon. They agreed on the way home that he was very Oriental-looking, that the failing evidently ran through their family and that it was disgusting of him to be living on his aunt.

Leslie did seem to have passed the fine line between staying and living. Mrs. Moysey was gratified, but she began to be anxious on his behalf. How would Japan be getting on? Oughtn't he to be going back there? She didn't like to ask him. The servants were becoming a little unsettled, the housemaid developed weeping-fits and had to be sent away. The cook took to burning the dinner, was severe when Mrs. Moysey mentioned it and talked about goings-on. Mrs. Moysey never ate much dinner, she was not interested in meals, but when she saw Leslie turn his food over and over with his fork, frown, push his plate away, she flushed pinker than ever, her eyes pricked with shame and vexation and in trembling tones she begged him to overlook it. The parlourmaid was present, she was what is called 'faithful', but the starch all over her person seemed to have entered into her soul. She whisked Leslie's plate away, as much as to say. 'Well, don't then!'

In spite of bad cooking and lack of social amenities Leslie, full of solicitude for his aunt's feelings, did seem inclined to stay on. His temper was very equable; if it couldn't be called sunny it was not at any rate bad. Mrs. Moysey was on this account all the more stupefied, shattered even, when creeping across the hall one morning on her way out to the shops she had a glimpse through the dining-room doorway, of Leslie distinctly 'put out'. Leslie, stiffly and whitely grinning, his teeth pressing away all the blood from his lip, was tearing a letter up into crumbs that fluttered slowly down on the light like a stage snowstorm. ' ――――her!' said Leslie softly, almost tenderly, 'The――! The – little――!'

'N-not bad news, Les, I hope?' said Mrs. Moysey.

Leslie borrowed ten pounds from his aunt and went up to London. He said goodbye – not, he hoped, for more than a day or two; he smiled more than usual, masked little smiles; a lingering terrible tenderness tinted his manner. She hoped, listening with locked hands pressed under her bosom to the slam of the door, that he'd taken enough money, had nice friends in town and hadn't (oh, why should she think so?) gone up to commit a murder! He hadn't left an address. Mrs. Moysey kept missing him terribly. She didn't come down that evening, she couldn't bear the look of the house. They brought her dinner up on a tray, and until nearly midnight the servants heard her playing the gramophone. Passers-by saw that the dining-room window was empty, or rather, that a table of plants, long displaced, had returned to it. Some waxy-leaved ferns and a dish of thick-fingered cacti, palpably crawling, carried on Leslie's tradition.

Three days later a young woman with hands in her mackintosh pockets stood looking up at the windows, made some irresolute movements and finally knocked. She and the parlourmaid stared at each other. Something in common between them, perhaps some potential resistance to Leslie the servant divined in her, travelled along the interchange. Resolutely anonymous, persisting that her name could mean nothing, she was admitted. Mrs. Moysey, informed through her door, replied in a voice more stopped-up and husky than usual, she wouldn't see anyone. The parlourmaid coughed. 'No, ma'am. I quite understand, ma'am.' Five seconds later, she was tapping again. 'The young lady did say it was urgent.'

'Nothing's as urgent as all that. I'm not dressed, I tell you. I can't see her now.'

'She said she could wait, ma'am.'

'What *does* she want?'

'You don't think it could be something about Mr. Leslie?'

'Don't be silly——' But soon Mrs. Moysey trailed over the drawing-room carpet her long purple skirts. The young woman, not having seen her before, did not perceive a new flame, a new dignity: Aunthood. She saw a pink lady, expansive, with a curious toppling expression from the Pompadour-curves of her coiffure and round, apprehensive eyes.

'Yes?' said Mrs. Moysey, without the formalities.

'Only, I came about your nephew——'

'Leslie – why, what's the matter?'

'Only that he's my husband. I. . . .'

They looked at each other in fearful dismay.

'I don't think, you know, that you ought to come here saying things like this. I don't know you.'

'I didn't suppose you would,' said the young woman, sarcastic but quavering. 'My husband's not here, I suppose?'

'My nephew's not here.'

'No, he wouldn't be. I was a fool to write.' She wriggled her shoulders angrily, so that the mackintosh rustled. 'My name's Emerald. Emerald Voles. Yes, it *is*. I've got two babies – I could show you. They're at the Station Hotel.'

'*Young* babies?' said Mrs. Moysey, crimson at this impropriety.

'Three and two – Aunt Moysey.'

Emerald had not a kind face. It was pinched, hard and aggressive; she spoke as though to call one Aunt were an insult. She might at least, Mrs. Moysey thought plaintively, try and be winning. Perhaps she was hungry. Perhaps, thought Mrs. Moysey, studying the concavities of the mackintosh, she hadn't much on underneath. She was not at all the type of girl one expected Leslie to fancy. Mrs. Moysey was on the point of saying, with perfect conclusiveness, 'You must be wrong about this. Leslie would never have had a wife without curves.'

It was funny of her to be wearing a mackintosh. Mrs. Moysey knew plenty of ladies who were not well off, but they didn't wear a mackintosh all day long. Perhaps she wanted to *look* deserted. It might be 'the confidence trick' – she had often been warned of it.

'Won't you take off your mackintosh?'

'Not till I've got something else to put on.'

'Oh, how dreadful! . . . Have you come from Japan?'

'Two years ago; just before Baby was born. I sold up most of my things to pay the passage. I had to get back to my mother – I needn't have hurried, it turned out; Mother died just after I started. Leslie was supposed to be coming back three months after; he didn't, of course, and I never got any money. I've never heard anything more of him. I wrote to the Consul where we'd been and to one or two other people, but that didn't come to anything; I suppose Leslie'd got in with some story first. So I just kept on living somehow and waited. Then the other day I got in touch with a lady I'd known out there. She was stiffish (showed what Leslie'd been saying), but she did let out that Leslie'd been sacked from his job and come home. She got me his address down here through the London branch of the firm – they'd been having some correspondence – I guessed he'd be with his Aunt Moysey,' Emerald added. With a (to Mrs. Moysey) ghastly kind of complacency she looked round the room and sat down.

Mrs. Moysey, surprised, as though struck by the aptness of the suggestion, sat down also. She hitched the top of herself further over her stays, adjusted the stays as inconspicuously as possible, released a long sigh from her body's constriction and said reflectively, 'Well, it's all been very unfortunate——'

'Very,' said Emerald pressingly.

'But I'm afraid I don't quite see how I——'

'If you'll wait for ten minutes I'll bring round the children at once. You might hesitate a minute or two over Daph, unless you'd seen her asleep or sulking, but there'll be no doubt at all about little Bobby.'

'But I'm not arranged for children,' wailed Mrs.

Moysey. Emerald (who, of course, could not help this) had left the room.

Ten minutes later, punctually, Emerald reappeared (Mrs. Moysey watched through the curtains) more wolfish than ever, nose to the wind up the street, pushing a folding go-cart. Little Bobby in a blue woolly cap walloped forward over the strap of the go-cart, and Daph, with little flax curls like bobbins at the back of a tilted bonnet, swung from her mother's left hand, tripping alongside. Before the go-cart had begun to bump up to the front door steps Mrs. Moysey, hot and cold from a sense of fatality, had acknowledged herself a great-aunt. The entrance clinched it. Daph, flattened against the maternal mackintosh, presented a coal-scuttle profile, but there was no doubt (as the snub-featured small dark face appeared round the mackintosh, was thrust forward – with cap snatched off from above and a dab at the curls – and presented itself square to the Aunt's gaze, embedded in jersey-collar and still swaying slightly from the arrested totter) about little Bobby.

'*There!* . . . ' whispered Mrs. Moysey, appalled by what Leslie had done.

'Little duckie,' she said later, tremulous. She sat well back in the big chair with knees jutting forward, disposed in this attitude almost in spite of herself, presenting a capable, destined and so far unoccupied lap. Daph, let out of her reefer, vivified by the removal of the bonnet, sheered round her in a constellation of pink bows, clambered up suddenly, nestled. A roll of the head, a listening pressure, the head heavy and warm and wonderfully round through the silver-fine hair . . . 'Little *duckie*!' . . . Bobby remained at a distance, he clutched and unclutched the arm of a chair with an air of having secured property. He lifted and lowered his eyelids, considering his great-aunt and sister sideways with a covert intentness. His father's look.

As Emerald had decreed, the children remained at Mrs. Moysey's (where they should do very well) while Emerald took back to London her persistent, charmless and unrelenting wifeliness to continue the search. She kept repeating, 'Oh, *I* haven't come down for anything. It's only the kiddies——' but finally she accepted a five-pound note and a Shetland coatee to wear under her mackintosh. She kissed the children in a queer, darting way, got away from them into the hall, but broke out into one husky noise like a bark when, there in the half-dark, she stumbled over the go-cart. 'It is *hard*,' she said, 'isn't it?' and dabbed at her eyes and the tip of her nose with savage efficiency.

'Dreadful,' agreed Mrs. Moysey, yet looked at the hat-rack where Leslie's check cap was still hanging with an irresponsible spasm of pity for Emerald's quarry.

'I said I'd be a good wife to my man when I took him,' said Emerald, 'and I've been a good wife to my man. Oh, I don't want anyone's pity. But I must say it does seem hard. And having to part from the kiddies——'

'Look, take my umbrella,' said Mrs. Moysey. 'I don't often use it. And if you want more money, write. And I'll write every day about Billy and Daph, I do promise. And if Leslie comes back——'

'Wire at once and keep him here!' shouted back Emerald, now half way down the steps.

'And I'll be sure and remember the name of those rusks,' panted Mrs. Moysey. 'And I'll teach them to pray for you every night——'

'They don't pray,' shouted Emerald. '*I* never got any good out of it.' She collided with someone, recoiled with a fierce exclamation and fled down the street.

The household, which had got so slowly and painfully into a gentleman's ways, must have gained thereby in elasticity, for it adapted itself without effort to Daph's and Bobby's. It absorbed the children. A bubble or two, some ripples that widened and vanished, then once more, above them, its unruffled surface of tranquil secretiveness. From the street, little repaid one's eager and close observation. They never came out. Now and then, their faces bobbed up over a window-sill, a fat hand was star-fished against a pane. Bars were screwed crosswise before an upstairs window, behind which, as autumn drew in, a light would appear about five o'clock. But no sooner was the light lit and the room with its bustling occupants tantalizingly vivid than the whole would be masked, triumphantly, by a crimson curtain. Neighbours looking out at the back could watch the couple, like young chickens, bowling about the garden under no visible supervision. Now and then the cook would come out and clap her hands at them; Mrs. Moysey's window creaked up for an admonition, then closed again. Her periodic sallies to the shops became more frequent, flurried, more awkwardly timed than ever; her load of parcels increased – she almost staggered. She offered no explanations, her house was not open to visitors. From the grim maids, less than ever communicative, nothing could be elicited.

Curiosity, starved by this silence, became suspicion. The children were there, unannounced, unapologized for; young children, still fresh from the impropriety of birth. The social circumstances that could have mitigated this impropriety remained unpublished, without doubt non-existent. Covertly someone had 'had' them. But who? It was not, physiologically alone, to be believed of Mrs. Moysey.

And further, discounting all this, was poor Mrs. Moysey a proper companion or guardian for children at all? She'd been odder than ever just recently; her actions, her inaction, were capable only of the most sinister interpretation. When she did not appear for a day or two that meant 'a bout', and when she came out two or three days in succession this was a sign that 'the failing', increasing its hold on her, demanded further and further supplies. Ladies with children shuddered to think what those poor little tots were exposed to; ladies without children, eager for social activity, demanded some interference: 'a rescue' it came to be called. Leslie was cited; even he, though a thoroughly nasty young fellow, had felt there were limits, had been crowded unwillingly out by the life in that house . . . *Poor* Mrs. Moysey, who might have been really so nice.

Poor Mrs. Moysey was indeed not herself at all. She lived in a long agitation, a flutter of happiness. Every morning a sense of the present, more poignant than sense of the future in youth or the past in age, shot through her waking bemusedness like a pang. She wrote every day to Emerald, the letters got shorter and shorter, so little of this was articulate, less still was proper for Emerald to know. Daph and Bobby were good as gold, as angels, their appetites were unexceptional, their insides like faultless clockwork. It had been all right giving them pheasant, hadn't it, thoroughly minced? They did seem to fancy it so – Daph was learning a little

poem to say to her Mummy. They asked every day for
their Mummy (she closed every letter with this convention), wasn't it sweet? The sweetness of Daph and Bobby
to Mummy-wards had, as a matter of fact, to be sounded
for more and more urgently. Mummy was less than a
name to them; she was forgotten. The more Mrs.
Moysey perceived this with exultation and horror, the
more conscientiously was Mummy evoked. But perhaps
Leslie's children partook of his feeling for softness, for
the curvilinear, for unrestraint. Mrs. Moysey with
scruples, with anguishing happiness, came to know that
Emerald was supplanted.

Daph and Bobby had not their father's delicacy and
were not to be impressed by the household with any
respect for Mrs. Moysey's door as a door. Having discovered these panels concealed their Aunt Moysey, they
drummed on them ceaselessly. At first Mrs. Moysey,
after a scuffle of preparation would come out like a flannel
and marabout cloud and envelop them; beneath her vast
impetus, trailing boas and shawls, they would be borne
along to the nursery, where she would endlessly play
with them. Then one day unexpectedly (to the breathless housemaid, incredibly) the door was held open a
crack and Daph and her brother oozed round it. This
privileged oozing-round became on wet mornings and all
afternoons a precedent. They were engulfed in the
innermost secrecy of that secret house. The housemaid
coming up with the coal, the parlourmaid with the tea-
tray, came as before to the door and no further, heard
conversation within, sometimes revelry, sometimes a
sociable silence. Implacably, still no one else was
admitted after the morning's dusting and sweeping, the
attention that grate and washstand required, were

finished. At six o'clock punctually Mrs. Moysey's bell rang; the children, bewildered as from Arabian enchantment, would be discovered outside on the mat.

About this time it was noticeable that their complexions, manners, tempers were beginning to deteriorate. In a week the deterioration had become more rapid and their appetites began to be affected. The maids, in consultation, hit on 'bowels', but laxatives did little for their complexions and only temporarily improved their moral tone. Daph turned from dinner after dinner, so did Bobby; 'lovely mince' and 'num-num bread and mink' appalled those children once so hungry and grateful; they fought and bit each other, and often before five o'clock had to be carried up, screaming, to bed. They became, it seemed incurably, yellow, spotty and demented. Their darlingness was in prolonged eclipse. Mrs. Moysey observed their condition anxiously, but when this was brought to her attention by the servants denied it with asperity.

'They're *little* children,' she explained to the cook. 'You're not used to little children. They have their little ups and downs – we all have. Try . . . try a little medicine.'

'I shouldn't care to give them any more medicine than what I have been giving them,' said the cook darkly. She looked hard at Mrs. Moysey. 'One would have thought,' she said, 'that they'd been having more than they should of what they shouldn't have to eat or drink. But of course that couldn't be . . . I sees to everything they eats and drinks myself. Everything.'

'Of course, of course,' agreed Mrs. Moysey, more than usually flustered.

'A good slapping's what I'd be disposed to try,' the

cook said, dispassionate as a goddess; 'they're getting spoilt, they are.'

'Never! I forbid you,' blazed out Mrs. Moysey, then subsided into wateriness. 'Do promise me you'll never think of that.'

'It's for you to say, ma'am,' said the cook formally.

Mrs. Moysey's visitors seemed fated to decline in popularity. For a long time cook talked of goings-on. Meanwhile, as day after day the screams of Daph and Bobby echoed down High Street, the rescue party mobilized itself and sent a deputation to the Vicar.

Emerald traced Leslie to a residential hotel in West Kensington where, as he pointed out to her, he had been living perfectly quietly, not doing anyone any harm. 'Then *you* come along,' he kept saying in a white heat of indignation which outblazed her own. He might have been a St. Anthony: she, from the air of spiritualized repudiation with which he viewed her untemptingness, the most persistent of temptations. He was proof, in speech and spirit, against everything but forgivingness; in the tentacles of this icy and arid forgivingness, which began to hover about him from the time of her entry, she did have him ultimately. She placed her submission before him, wherever he turned, like a plate of unfinished cold mutton before a refractory child; he was dogged by her constancy as his children were, elsewhere, being dogged by the cook with their platefuls of lovely mince. She unceasingly talked of the kiddies. 'It does seem hard they shouldn't have a Daddy. Bobby's beginning to talk now; 'Dad-dad' he keeps saying. He can't understand, you see. Of course I've never told them anything, Leslie; I'd hate them to know——'

That plate of cold mutton was planked down before him again.

Leslie had not been alone in the hotel in West Kensington; he was there with a nice Mrs. Moss he had met coming home from Japan. His delicacy, his consequent eagerness to avoid an encounter between Emerald and Mrs. Moss – who might come in at any moment – played into Emerald's hands. Her entente with his Aunt Moysey clinched matters. His aunt must have 'taken things' wonderfully well or she'd never have taken the children. There would be needed, to re-win her entirely, nothing but a flourish of conjugality which he was resigned to perform. 'If you've squared things,' he questioned cautiously, 'if you're quite *certain* you've squared things?' Where the Voles as a *ménage* were concerned, Emerald had certainly; for himself, she said, he must look to his charms. 'Oh then, that's all right,' sighed out Leslie, lay down like a sacrifice on the bed and let Emerald pack. She packed up his bag for him, summoned a taxi, settled his bill (wouldn't poor Mrs. Moss be surprised when she had to settle her own!) and removed him forthwith. It wasn't half bad, Leslie thought, leaning back with closed eyes in the taxi while Emerald totted up her accounts in a notebook and counted her change, to be going about with a wife of one's own once again. One did need looking after. Mrs. Moss, for instance, never did anything for him; she expected, in fact, the contrary: she was one of those clinging things.

In the train, however, Leslie began to feel indignant again with Emerald for her lack of motherly feeling. Having revolved the matter, uncertain if it were worth the effort of speech, he said dreamily, 'You know best, of course, but I must say I should never have dreamed of leaving young children where you've left yours.'

'It seemed to me proper,' said Emerald snappily.

'Oh well, if you've no prejudice,' Leslie said, raising his eyebrows. 'You know about Auntie, of course?'

'More than she knew about you.'

'Her habits?'

'Her *habits*?'

Leslie raised an elbow and dropped his head back in an expressive gesture. 'Tipples like hell,' he said mournfully. 'Poor old dear!' He had made more friends locally than Mrs. Moysey supposed.

'You don't *mean* that? Oh, Leslie . . . the horrid old creature! She looked so respectable – how could I know?'

'Dreadful, isn't it?' agreed Leslie. 'I must say, she keeps up appearances wonderfully. Never touches a drop at table. I daresay the kids will be all right. Bit scared, probably. Makes an impression on young children, that kind of thing. Still, I daresay they'll be all right.'

'I shall go mad,' said Emerald, looking grim and determined. After all this . . . her kiddies . . . But Leslie had gone to sleep.

Emerald shot past the parlourmaid into the hall; Leslie came in after her. He was much relieved at finding his good check cap still on the hat-rack; he took it down, looked at the lining and hung it up again. 'Home again, Phyllis,' he said to the parlourmaid affably. But Phyllis headed him into the impersonal dusky drawing-room as though he had been a caller. She jerked up the blinds and knelt down with a creak at the knee-joints to put a match to the fire. 'I'll tell the mistress,' said Phyllis, and looked round the room rather insultingly, as though taking an inventory of everything in there.

But Emerald barred her exit. 'Where are the children?'

'I can't say, I'm sure, ma'am. Probably up in the mistress's room.'

As bad as that! If Emerald lacked the allurements, she was complete with every instinct proper to her sex. She charged upstairs and though on the first floor, still strange to her, might well have been at a loss, was attracted unerringly to those varnished panels, the impassable shining discretion of Mrs. Moysey's door. Justified by maternity, she put an ear to the keyhole. She heard the double voice of her children upraised querulously, a silence, a short groan of acquiescence, the squeak of released chair springs, then Mrs. Moysey moving immensely about in reluctance, distraction, uncertainty – or was it sheer lack of control? For some moments of keenest anxiety Emerald listened, then rap-a-tapped. *'Who's* there?' said the choked voice. Rap-a-tap-tap, insisted Emerald, 'Well, what *do* you want?' Rap-tap-tap.

Mrs. Moysey came to the other side of the door, breathing urgently. With a gurgle she caught her breath back; she and Emerald listened intently for one another. Then encouraged by some misinterpreted quality in Emerald's silence she stealthily slid back the bolt. Emerald's fingers had crept to the door knob, she wrenched this round smartly, flung her weight on to the door and burst in, rebounding sideways from against Mrs. Moysey and knocking over a screen which had concealed the room.

Emerald's children looked up at her out of a coloured earthquake-city. Unnerved by her manner they turned to retreat; gilt, flowered and brightly pictorial boxes scrunched with the unresistance of cardboard under their wildly-placed feet. They evacuated, with shaken majesty, an empire of chocolate boxes. A kind of road system of ribbons twisted over the carpet; a round lid with a pussy cat's head looking out of a horse-shoe bowled away from them, spun like a platter at Emerald's feet and was still. The boxes were very artistic and striking. Flower-sprays or Zoo scenes, dragons in synthetic embroidery, 'The Angelus', 'Lady Hamilton', girls' heads in the popular manner, the Tower of London by moonlight, hunting scenes, the Prince of Wales, 'The Monarch of the Glen', and more lids with an opulent restraint in their lettering were, with the boxes they covered, built up into towers and bridges or arranged in patterns. Others, rejected or not yet made use of, were scattered profusely.

'Oh, it's you, is it, Emerald?' said Mrs. Moysey at last. 'Are you in such a hurry?'

Emerald was as nearly as possible shattered. The brave little woman felt deprived and beaten as never before. She couldn't collect herself and felt she could never forgive Mrs. Moysey for having betrayed her.

'I came up to tell you,' she said in a voice dank with injury, 'I found Leslie this morning. I felt it was right you should know.'

'Indeed! Well, I'm glad,' Mrs. Moysey said distantly. 'As a matter of fact,' she continued, surprised at herself for feeling resentful and still more surprised at feeling resentment gain ground in her, 'you've given me quite a shock. I'm not strong; I should have thought that

you'd know that: you've frightened the children, too . . .
There, hush, little darlings . . . There, Daffles, hush . . .
Isn't that a funny Mummy? That was Mummy's surprise, wasn't it? Mummy came in and said "Peep-bo",
didn't she? "Peep-bo", she said.'

The great-aunt went down on her knees with sur-
prising agility and held her arms out over the littered
floor. The children fled into them, buried their faces
like ostriches, shaking with sobs. The blonde and the
dark head pressed deeper into the crimson capaciousness;
Mrs. Moysey, closing her arms with protective finality,
gently and gingerly rocked from the knees. 'There –
there, Daph.' Daph peeped up across the protective
shoulder, saw Emerald put out a hand, ducked her face
down again and redoubled her screams.

'I'm afraid you'll have to keep back for a minute or
two,' said Mrs. Moysey. 'They're still rather frightened.
I'm used to their ways, you see.'

'What a *thing* to say to a mother!' Emerald marvelled.

Mrs. Moysey, looking down, was immersed in a business of stroking, murmuring, dabbing with her handkerchief, kissing, dabbing again.

'Something's very much wrong with their tempers,'
continued Emerald, 'they never did this with me!'
She sat down at a distance, repudiating the relatives
huddled like Christians in the arena, and began to count
the chocolate boxes. When she had come to fifty-eight
she noticed that the doors of a wardrobe were open
and that a far greater number of boxes were stacked
up inside. She gave up in despair. It was all very cosy
in here, one big chair – not more, for one sat at ease
here in uncorseted freedom and wasn't driven to roam,
constricted uneasily, questing for comfort – a table

spread with manuscript books, a white bearskin tinged
with firelight, a drum-shaped stool at the edge of the
rug. On the stool, one more box with the lid off – not
empty. The box was about the size of a dinner-plate
and so far only a dozen chocolates were missing; the
rest were arranged in a lovely design like a rose. They
looked to Emerald the sort that would only be given to
very immoral ladies by very rich men. They were now
being eaten, there wouldn't be any more left. Emerald
went back through her thoughts, testing every connection, her eye travelled back to the wardrobe, the town
on the floor.

'Have you eaten all these, Aunt Moysey?' she asked,
with the simplicity of a Riding Hood.

Aunt Moysey looked up at her over the children's
heads. 'Well yes, I suppose I must have. One time and
another . . .' She looked round at her boxes, between
wonder and a genuine gratification.

Emerald's rigid attention made further demands.

'They do rather mount up, I suppose. The fact is,'
she went on, gathering speed and a certain recklessness,
'I don't throw my boxes away . . . They are so artistic,
I think – well, look at that sunset, for instance; you
couldn't buy a picture like that for quite a large sum if
you asked for it in a gallery. I've made quite a little
collection, haven't I, all these years? As a matter of fact,
I look at them quite a lot.'

'Did you ever show them to Leslie?'

'Oh no. I mean, he'd have thought me so silly, you
know. Gentlemen never seem to me to have quite the
same feeling for beautiful things. Do you think so?'

'I can't say; I've never had any – beautiful things, I
mean.'

'I know, I *know*,' said Mrs. Moysey, 'that's what makes it so terrible of me, gratifying my fancies. That's why I'm so ashamed. Think of the little children now, starving all over the world! When I think of them I hardly know what to do.'

Her children had stopped crying and were struggling and pushing against her breast. She opened her arms and relinquished them, looking after them for a moment or two. Then she looked at their mother with a startlingly personal brightness, a flash of the self through her fumbling secretiveness like the flash of a rare shy bird through an overgrown thicket. The look glanced off from the obdurate face of Emerald, cold with thought. But she was tasting, perhaps for the first time, the sweetness of self-betrayal.

'So few people would understand,' she continued. 'It does sound terrible, doesn't it? I'd hate people – Leslie or you or the neighbours – to think ill of me. I've always been most careful. That's what's wonderful about children, isn't it; they understand. Bobby and Daph enter into everything – why, I'm even reading them my book.'

'Oh, I'm afraid you couldn't expect them to understand *that*. Are you writing a book?'

Mrs. Moysey looked at Emerald sideways. It was as though the bird poised in the thicket, then with queer cry darted into the open. 'Oh yes, I wrote a good deal – a life of myself. Well, not my life strictly, that wouldn't be interesting to me; I do touch things up here and there. There are so many points in a life when things so nearly . . . I don't see any harm myself in putting those sorts of things in – well, what is just one's life in *itself*, if you come to think of it? Then there are some things, of

course, I leave out. Well, you wouldn't expect to find
in a book about anyone's indigestion . . . Daph and Bob
are loving the story, they listen entranced——'

Here Mrs. Moysey had to break off, for Emerald's
failure to listen had become as positive as an interruption.
The eyes of the mother, devoid of illusion, sharp with
practical understanding, had meanwhile been ferreting
out the handkerchief which, lately employed in the
aunt's ministrations, was now concealed in the fold of
Mrs. Moysey's lap. The handkerchief, crumpled and
clammy, was blotched a dissolute pinky-brown. Mrs.
Moysey, attention arrested, also looked down at the
handkerchief. Emerald's gaze wheeled sideways. Her
children, puffy from crying, were reassembling their
city. Daph placed the Prince of Wales on The Angelus,
Bobby knocked him off again. They snarled at each
other. Thick brown stains, dispersed from their mouths
by the dabbing of Mrs. Moysey, echoed over their faces.
A thin brown dribble of chocolate ran down Daph's
frock.

'What have they had?' exclaimed Emerald. '*How much
of that have they eaten?*' There ensued an appalled
silence, the hollow tumbling of boxes. The children
looked up at each other, then at their aunt. The three
were banded together by this interchange, which
excluded Emerald finally like the slam of a door.
Emerald quivered all over. Her thin hands quivered,
locked in her lap, the movement ran up to her shoulders,
so piteously set in a decent woman's bravado. She
jerked her chin backwards with a convulsive movement,
as though lassoed from behind.

'They're never allowed any! They *know* they're
never allowed any! *You* know they're never allowed

any. No wonder they're sick and poisoned and don't know their own mother. Sold!' said Emerald slowly, 'that's what I've been!'

There did indeed seem nobody she could trust.

'*Hush!*' cried out Mrs. Moysey, then put her two hands to her mouth for very horror.

'Stolen!' said Emerald. 'That's what they've been . . . my own children.'

She said no more, for her virtue, her indignation more awful than eloquence mounted into a wave that, dwarfing her, even, toppled over the room. As though the weight of that wave were to crash down both women put out their arms for the menaced children.

Bobs and Daffie, tottering to their feet in alarm, looked this and that way, then with one movement flung themselves both, face down, into Mrs. Moysey's lap and clutched and clung there, you would have said in desperation.

'There . . .' said Emerald, almost gently, and began the clik-cluk-cluk of a dry sobbing.

You would have said there was no place, no home in the world for decent women.

And Mrs. Moysey – most unwilling victor – half clutching the children to her because Mother was so frightening, half pushing them from her because Mother was so lonely, poor Mrs. Moysey – most unconvinced voluptuary – did not know where to look. . . .